LOKI

A NOVEL

M.G. FARIJA

For Ahmed. . . .

I believe that legends and myths are largely made of 'truth.'

— J.R.R. TOLKIEN

Edited by Robin Schroffel

mgfarija.com

PROLOGUE

Myth ['mith] *noun*
    1 a: a usually traditional story of ostensibly historical events
that serves to unfold part of the worldview of a people or explain
a practice, belief, or natural phenomenon

MYTHS ARE PECULIAR THINGS. They are often nothing more than the product of an all too imaginative and superstitious people's attempt to make sense of what appears to be senseless. More often than not, the roots of myth are fictitious. However, sometimes, the line between history and fiction becomes blurred. Stories of people long forgotten transform into tales of giants and gods. Take, for instance, the story of Thor, Odin, Loki, and the land of Yggdra.

No one is sure of Yggdra's precise location. Many theories persist, all of them wrong. Another point that lacks clarity is why and how the Nordic peoples took the tales of Yggdra as their own, mythologizing and deifying them. But that is beside the point.

The land of Yggdra had nine provinces, known as realms. Niflheim, a land of the bitterest cold imaginable, lay to the north. To the south was Helheim, where lifeless deserts stretched as far as the horizon.

Svartalfheim and Alfheim, north of Helheim, did not occupy themselves with the business of their neighbors. While they engaged with them in trade, they did not partake in their quarrels, politics, and wars. Instead, they busied themselves with their crafts.

When armies went to battle, it wasn't uncommon for the smiths of Svartalfheim to arm both sides. After all, they were the finest weapon makers in the nine realms. The people of Alfheim had a different, but no less profitable, craft: poetry. The art of flattery is perfected in poetry, and the royals of Yggdra were more than willing to part with their money to hear it.

While the two kingdoms enjoyed enviable riches, Midgard, located at the heart of Yggdra, was by far the wealthiest of the nine realms—a fact unknown to all other nations (and even to most of Midgard's own populace). None were rich, and none were poor. Unlike all other inhabited realms, Midgard had no king. The land ruled. Redwoods, thick, tall, and firm, packed its forests. Fields of wheat and barley stretched miles on end. Oxen and muskoxen moved freely through the grasslands. The people—humblefolk, some called them—grew their crops, reared their cattle, traded with their neighbors, and kept to themselves.

Fortune had blessed the humblefolk with profitable borders. To Midgard's north was Jotunheim, a land where nothing much grew due to an ever-present winter. To its west was Vanaheim, a nation no less fruitful than Midgard but whose people lacked the wherewithal to till the soil. To the south was Asgard, whose agriculture was self-sustaining but whose elites preferred exotic tastes (in food and women at least).

The monarchs of Asgard, Jotunheim, and Vanaheim found that suppressing internal conflict was best achieved through war with one's neighbors. As long as the masses directed their discontent toward the 'other,' they would not pay attention to problems of a more local nature.

War between the three became the norm. Thousands died to

2

claim a mile of territory only for it to be reclaimed threefold the next year. And so the dance continued, year after year, decade after bloody decade, century after century. Along the way, someone (no one is sure who) forgot it was a dance, a meaningless spectacle, and believed the lie. Ignited by an unknown spark, the kingdoms of Asgard and Vanaheim found themselves engaged in the most destructive war the world had ever known. Jotunheim, however, remembered the dance for what it was and retreated into isolationism.

Then, something unexpected happened. King Borr of Asgard called for peace. "Peace through unity. Unity through blood." To cement their alliance, Asgard and Vanaheim declared war on Jotunheim.

The campaign was short, swift, and bloody. While the Jotunns would've been able to deflect the advances of Asgard and Vanaheim individually, the united army was a force hitherto unknown. Villages burned, towns lay in ruins, and cities were leveled, all in the name of peace.

On the hills of Geirrod, the Jotunns made their last stand. They ambushed the Aesir and Vanir armies. Hundreds fell as arrows rained down from the sky. Fire pierced through the snow. Swords painted the white below crimson. Through sheer numbers, the armies of Asgard and Vanaheim claimed victory, though the toll was heavy. Nearly half of the Aesir's army perished, and for every Vanir that survived, seven did not.

"What would you have me do?" said Njord, king of Vanaheim, as burning funeral pyres illuminated the night sky. "What would you have history write of me?"

"Your men have suffered enough," Borr replied. "Too many mothers have lost their sons. Too many wives have lost their husbands."

"You would have me retreat? To return to Vanaheim without avenging the lives of my men?" Njord paced back and forth, passing his hands through what little hair he had left. "You want me to stay back while you sack Utgard. No, no, that's not going to happen. I will not have history remember me as a coward. What men I have left will fight."

"These are not the words of a wise king," Odin said.

"And who spoke to you, boy?" Njord barked.

"Speak to my son that way again and I will have your head," said Borr, in the manner in which a person says 'pass the salt.' "Peace through unity. Unity through blood," he muttered under his breath. "Your men fall back, Njord. You have no say in this matter. Your men will remember you as merciful, and your women will thank you for the lives of their sons and husbands. Disobey this command and history will remember that wise King Njord fell fighting the Jotunns on the hills of Geirrod. Is that clear?"

As the Vanir army marched homewards, the army of Asgard pushed north to the fortress of Utgard. Fortified by walls several meters thick and too tall to scale, the fortress of Utgard had never been taken. On the council of his son, Odin, Borr ordered the Aesir army to surround the castle, but remain far enough away to stay out of arrow's range.

For three bitter months, they starved them out. And then one night, a few hours before dawn, fire rained down on the inhabitants of the castle. Archers were struck down as they rushed to the walls. Utgard's gate, which had stood for over a thousand years, was burnt to cinders. The Aesir army flooded the streets, killing anything and anyone in sight. Swords fell upon mothers holding their children in their arms. Homes burned, while those inside suffocated. "Where is your king?" roared Borr as his war hammer cracked the skull of a boy no older than five. "Where is the one who will defend you?"

As the fortress burned, Farbauti, king of Jotunheim, lay in his bedchamber and awaited his fate. Under his reign, the land was prosperous. But within mere months, the cities and towns which had flourished under his rule lay in ashes. Screams echoed through the room for hours, followed by a deafening silence, and an oddly polite knock on the door.

He opened the door to his bedchamber to find a man covered in blood. The man had long red hair. The chainmail armor he wore was battle-worn, and in his left hand was a war hammer. Behind him was a man far younger but of similar complexion, armed with a broadsword.

"Come in," Farbauti said, motioning toward the wooden table at the center of the room. Borr and Odin entered and shut the door behind themselves. "Have a seat," said Farbauti, pulling out a chair.

"Your men die fighting while you sit here," Borr said. "As I suspected—a broken coward through and through."

"This isn't a battle," Farbauti said. "Tell me, oh brave king, how much of that blood on your armor belongs to women and children?" Borr remained silent. "What was built over a lifetime, you've destroyed in but days. Why? What was Jotunheim's crime?"

"This conquest is a symbol of unity, nothing more. I would not have you take it personally," Borr said. "But your imminent death will bring an end to the killing. You have my word."

"I would have given my life to you freely had I known that my people would have been spared. Do what you must."

"Son, would you honor me?" Borr said to Odin. And with that, Odin drove his sword through Farbauti's throat.

"It is over," Borr said as he stood up to leave. But as the two were about to exit the room, a small whimper echoed from the cabinet in the corner. As Borr approached it, he could hear shallow breathing on the other side. He outstretched his hand to Odin, who obliged by giving his father the sword. Without a word, Borr plunged the sword into the door at eye level. He took a deep breath and opened the door, revealing the dead woman and the sleeping baby in her arms. The red liquid dripping from the mother's forehead woke the child, who was no more than a few months old. Borr pried it from its dead mother's arms and did something Odin did not anticipate. He wept. As he held the baby in his arms, he cried—cried for the meaninglessness of it all, for the things he'd seen, and most of all, for the things he'd done.

Sandwiched between Svartalfheim and Asgard was Muspelheim, the smallest of the nine realms. Although bountiful and beautiful, Muspelheim remained uninhabited. Its only notable attraction was the mountain.

Mount Surt was the highest point in the nine realms. Many tried to climb it, most failing, and a sizable number dying in the attempt. Yet every other year, Borr climbed it faster than any had done before —or after.

The mountain's winds were colder than he remembered, or perhaps they were as cold as they had ever been. What was once a comfortable journey, nothing more than a periodic display of his physical fitness, was now an ordeal which he half regretted embarking on. Only the view made the pain searing through his joints worth it.

Though in his late eighties, he did not look a day older than sixty. Twelve years of peace had aged him more than the previous thirty (the threat of war is a marvelous incentive to maintain peak physical fitness).

"I can feel it," Borr said, grabbing at the falling snow. "The call from the great beyond. My fathers. They call me. They welcome me. They tell me it is time. I must admit, I'm afraid. What mercy will be given to a soul that has killed as many as I have? What hope of forgiveness is left for me? I am cursed, my son. Cursed by the screams of thousands. Cursed by the silence. Cursed by the price I paid."

"Father, perhaps we should turn back."

"You fear the mountain has driven me mad? No, my son. I see clearly. I have given nothing to this world but death and blood."

"You have given this world peace."

"Peace," Borr muttered to himself. "Peace." He turned and locked eyes with Odin. "Peace built on the back of an innocent child."

"The Jotunns will not attack us if we have their rightful heir."

"He's a child!" Borr's body shuddered, battling the freezing gale. "A child," he repeated. "A child."

"What would you ask of me, Father?"

"Why did I save that child?" Borr said, not to Odin but himself. "I didn't save him to lock him up. Why did I save that child?" He grabbed Odin by the shoulders. "Be a better man than me."

6

"You would have me free the Jotunn?" Odin said.

"I would have you free him. I would have you take him as your brother, your equal. And in time, I would have you love him as a brother."

<hr />

Long winding corridors of rock lay at the base of the castle, a labyrinth many found confusing in design. Stores of weapons, grain, salted meat, and mead made up the bulk of the basement. One corridor, the darkest and dampest of the lot, was allocated for prisoners, enemies of the crown. The peace, which had kept for twelve years, meant all of the cells remained empty. All but one.

He's far too smart for his age, Mimir thought. Loki, son of Farbauti and Laufey, the true heir to Jotunheim, whose age was somewhere between twelve and thirteen, had spent the previous night studying the grammatical evolution of Alfhen poetry. Three books, each of them as thick as a fist, lay beside the mattress on the floor.

"All last night?"

"All of them," Loki said proudly.

"And what did you think?"

The boy shrugged his shoulders. "Mansur had a few stories I liked." Loki patted the thickest of the three books. "The one about Horod and the Temple Spire. The great fire of Otune. Most of it didn't make sense. The structures and forms the Alfhen stick to . . . it makes everything predictable. I mean, if you know where a poem's going, what's the fun in it? The old ones are the best. The new ones—" He scrunched his little face into a ball. "—not so much."

The boy's face was far too gaunt, an emaciated, skeletal frame. Nevertheless, he smiled. For years the boy did not understand his predicament. He didn't complain. But he knew little boys were not raised in dungeons, fed nothing more than scraps, and visited (almost) every day by an old man. For years he asked, "Why am I here?" to which Mimir would always reply with a solemn expression and a sigh.

Then, one day, Mimir presented the boy with a book, *The Aesir Vanir War* by Mimir Odin Counsel.

"You wrote this?" Loki gasped.

"I did. And let me tell you a secret." He leaned in close to the boy. "Do you know who's the most important person in this story?"

"I don't know."

"You," Mimir said.

Loki snatched the tome from Mimir's lap, turning toward the final pages. He passed his fingers through the long lines of names and paused when he reached his own. "Loki," he said, "son of Farbauti and Laufey, the true heir to Jotunheim."

"You're a king, my son."

"And that's why I'm here," Loki said, motioning his head toward the endless grey.

"Not quite." Mimir bit his tongue. "Never mind—ramblings of an old fool. Now, Loki, I need your help. The book you're holding in your hand, I'm supposed to give it to the king in a week. It took me a bit longer with this one."

"You wrote other ones?!"

"Yes, many, but that's beside the point. Apart from me, you're the fastest reader in this entire blasted castle."

"Don't have much else to do."

"Yes, point taken. I need you to read this book, as fast as you can, and tell me if I made any writing mistakes. It's a thick one, so, oh, about three days should be enough for you."

Loki didn't sleep that night. Given what he'd learned, how could he sleep? He grieved that night, as best a child of nine (or ten) could grieve. Grieved for his father, resigned to death. Grieved for his mother, who died holding him in her arms.

The next morning, when Mimir entered Loki's cell, the old man was not greeted with the usual smile. Instead, Loki lobbed the book directly at Mimir's forehead as hard as his scrawny little arms could. The force of the blow knocked the old man off his feet.

"He killed them!" Loki said, his eyes red. "He killed them all!" The boy flung his fists at the old man. Mimir grabbed him, pulled him close, and hugged him as tightly as he could.

"I know, my son, I know," said the old man as the boy cried in his arms. Not another word was said that day; Mimir just held the boy and let him weep.

As they sat on the wet cobblestone floor all those years later, discussing Alfhen poetry, the pitter-patter of footsteps echoed through the corridors. The boy with red hair was much taller than Loki, broader, and stronger than most his age. "Father wants to see him," Thor said, pointing at Loki.

Loki found himself unintentionally motioning his body backward. "It's alright, my son," Mimir said, putting a hand on Loki's lap. "Perhaps Odin will finally heed the words of his counsel."

The throne room was far more humble than Loki imagined. It was old and in dire need of renovation. He gripped Mimir's hand tight as they walked down the long and uncomfortable walkway. Statues of kings, princes, warriors, and saints adorned the edges of the hall, a sizable number of which were missing limbs and noses. Odin sat to the right of Borr, the seat that Thor would one day inherit, and to Borr's left was an empty chair, one that was far less inviting than the two to its right: the king's counsel's chair. Cylin, Borr's counsel, would have sat there, but due to his death three years ago, was unable to. The wind kept the seat warm for Mimir, who would lay claim to it the moment Odin became king.

"Mimir tells me that your kindness is only surpassed by your wit," Borr said, his voice stronger than his body. "Do you know of your lineage?" Loki nodded. "Then tell me, child, why did I spare you on that fateful night twelve years ago?"

Loki looked toward Mimir for approval but found the old man's eyes fixed upon the king. "Peace, sire. Jotunheim would not attack Asgard as long as the heir to—"

"No," Borr roared, interrupting the boy. "No. I did not spare you for peace. Jotunheim lays leaderless and in ashes. It is certainly not a threat. I spared you for mercy. As you cried in your dead mother's arms, I could not find it in myself to leave you to die. Though I carried you to my home, I couldn't bear the sight of you. In your eyes, I saw them. All the eyes I forced shut, for nothing more than the crime of existence. I am not a good man. But perhaps my soul was the price I had to pay to ensure peace in the nine realms. Come closer, child; let me take a better look at you. My eyes aren't what they once were." Loki did as Borr asked. "Just a bag of bones," Borr whispered to himself.

"I held you in my arms and contemplated killing you, and it was at that moment that I knew what I had become. Not the brave king who led his people to peace, not even human, but a murderer of children, a monster. Today, here, in this hall, I shall hope to do what I should have done all those years ago."

Odin stepped forward, brandishing a small knife. Loki's breath quickened. He closed his eyes, waiting for it all to end. Mimir gave him a little prod, forcing him to open his eyes.

"I share with you my blood, Loki," Odin said, passing the knife through the palm of his hand, "that we may be brothers, and you an adopted son to my father, and swear never to harm you."

Loki outstretched his palm and tried not to wince.

PART I
ASGARD

CHAPTER ONE

ONE CANNOT FATHOM the seemingly insignificant choices that go on to change one's life. What might appear at the time to be an action carrying little weight may go on to transform the world.

Loki motioned away from the bar, trying his best to ignore the putrid stench, not knowing the significance of what was about to transpire. The Horned Helm had, once upon a time, been a reputable and respected establishment. Time, as it often does, stripped the Helm of every strip of decency. Under normal circumstances, Loki would have advocated avoiding the tavern, but after six months on the road, all he wanted was a stiff drink and a warm bed. A quiet discomfort took him as he placed the two tankards on the table.

Loki knew the look in Thor's eyes all too well. It was a look that often preceded events that would land them in more trouble than Loki cared for. This time was no different. Before the day was over, he and Thor would kill a man and set in motion events that would reshape the fabric of Yggdra.

Thor dragged the tankard toward himself, took a sizable gulp of mead, and scratched his forehead with his index and middle fingers.

"No," Loki said before Thor could form a coherent thought.

"I said nothing."

"Whatever that voice in your head is whispering, shut it up."

"I said nothing!"

"Don't think anything either. That's my job."

Thor wiped the golden liquid from his thick auburn beard. "Remind me again why we're here."

"Really?" Loki growled, knowing where the conversation was headed.

"Really."

"To travel the realm and live among the people, for a king that does not know his people is no king at all."

Thor motioned to the barmaid for another tankard. "So what have we seen so far? We've seen food supply issues in Tilgrad and Pildur, the strikes in Milonheim, blight in the east, trade disputes with Svartalfheim. Now, these are your concerns, not mine."

"You're going to be king, not me," Loki replied.

"Yes, and a wise king knows his limits. Matters of trade, wealth distribution . . . concerning these matters, I will always defer to you."

"Who says I'm always going to be there to be deferred to?"

"You're my counsel. It's your job to be deferred to. You're good at what you do. You're in the chain of command. Mimir defers to you. Advises Odin. And Odin ignores both of you. It's hilarious, but back to my point. The things that you're good at, I'm not. As the Master of Arms, I still can't answer the most fundamental question of my job. Can my people defend themselves? Can you answer that question?"

"No."

"No, I thought not."

"I didn't mean no like that, you idiot. I mean no, wherever your thinking is headed, no. Don't go there."

Loki had been tense from the moment they entered Sirhilm, knowing the town would not encourage Thor's wisest tendencies. Odin had long banned the use of lethal force in Sirhilm's fighting pits, to dissuade the populace's baser proclivities. Instead, the pits—which were hardly pits, more akin to small dilapidated arenas spread throughout Sirhilm's southern province—functioned on what they called a 'champion system.' A 'champion' would fight any man who declared himself to a bare-knuckled brawl. The first man to draw blood or force their opponent to the ground would then be anointed 'champion.' 'Champions' didn't remain champions long. Tired after the first round, they would often fall quickly during the next.

Sirhilm's fighting pits, Loki believed, would prove too great a temptation for Thor. Those who entered the pits would not pose a serious physical threat to Thor. Loki's concern was, in fact, the opposite.

As soon as Thor had learned to walk, Odin made sure he could fight. Knights, generals, and sell-swords would travel from all nine realms to train the young prince. (On two separate occasions Odin had even made arrangements for Jotunn swordsmen to travel to Asgard—in exchange for protection and a substantial monetary reward, of course.) Though proficient in hand-to-hand combat, archery, and swordsmanship, Thor's weapon of choice was the war hammer.

As time went on, it became apparent to everyone that Thor was, by far and away, the fiercest warrior in the nine realms. He was tall, with an imposing broad, muscular build. Despite his size, Thor was devilishly fast on his feet, catching the strikes of Asgard's greatest fighters midair and forcing them down before they could even evaluate their next blow.

Thor's skill had gained high repute throughout the realms, with many traveling from as far away as Alfheim to spar with him. Such fame was, most assuredly, problematic to Thor and Loki's mission, which relied on (as Odin would continuously remind them) anonymity.

Long ago, under the orders of his father, Odin had ventured into the land under the name Grimnir. His mission, or so everyone was told, was to live amongst the people he would one day rule. He was to learn about the difficulties they faced and to understand how they thought. As Borr told him, "A king must know his people. For a king that does not know his people is no king at all."

It was now Thor's turn to embark on this mission. However, Odin knew of Thor's reliance on Loki and so decreed Loki join Thor, much to Loki's chagrin. The most essential prerequisite for their mission's success was to remain unnoticed. "A king is but a man," Odin would say. "He eats, shits, and pisses like the rest of them. People seem to forget that."

Loki feared that the moment people saw Thor fight, they would deduce precisely who he was. Alas, he resigned himself to failure the moment Thor said, "Why am I trying to justify myself to you? It's not like you can stop me." Thor gulped down his drink in an instant, ordered another before Loki could mutter a single word, slurped it down, and walked out the door, leaving Loki to foot the bill.

The pits were just as Loki had imagined. Rickety wooden structures, a small arena in the middle, and a viewing gallery that could accommodate no more than fifty people. It wasn't hard to find Thor, who was already yelling and hollering in the middle of the arena, calling out for a challenger as the former 'champion' held his blood-soaked head in his arms, in far too much pain to cry.

A guard stood at the gate, loosely holding a spear in one hand and a sword in the other. He checked the oncoming challenger for weapons and allowed him to pass. The challenger found himself greeted with a haymaker the moment he entered and was ungracefully dragged back out of the arena as fast as he'd walked in. Thor winked at Loki, noticing him in the small gallery.

Three challengers entered. Each regretted doing so. Thor allowed the first to strike at him, dodging each blow more gracefully than any man his size had any right to do. Once the man tired out, Thor kicked his feet up from underneath him, causing him to fall flat onto his face. With the second challenger, Thor was far less forgiving. The man lunged at Thor's feet, attempting to tackle him down. In turn, Thor grabbed him by the neck, lifted him, and sent him flying face-first into the arena's short wooden walls. The third challenger was a rotund man. Thor felt that it would not be honorable to inflict too much pain upon him. He allowed the fat man to charge him, stepped aside, and outstretched his leg. The man landed with a thud.

"Are we done yet?" called Loki from the gallery.

Thor waved his hand in a manner that communicated, "I can hear you, I just don't care."

The next man to enter the arena was considerably larger than the four that preceded him. He had long jet-black hair tied in a ponytail, arms as thick as tree trunks, and a scar that went from forehead to shoulder. He circled Thor. The smile on Thor's face disappeared. He stepped back, readying himself for the onslaught to come.

Sensing something was wrong, the guard stationed at the arena's entrance held his sword tight in both hands, mistakenly leaving his spear leaning against the arena's wall.

"For Jotunheim!" cried the man with the scar as he lunged toward Thor. Thor moved aside, knowing that blocking such a blow would be useless. But the man with the scar anticipated this. He revealed two small blades hidden between his fingers and in one motion, threw one at the guard and lunged at Thor once more, driving the dagger deep into Thor's thigh.

Unthinkingly, Loki leaped from the gallery into the arena, ran past the guard's motionless body, and grabbed the spear.

"Your father took my son," said the man with the scar as he walked toward Thor, who was struggling to stand, blood flowing freely from the wound. "I'm only returning the favor."

The spear pierced the man with the scar's shoulder as soon as the words left his lips, forcing him to the ground.

Finding the strength to lift himself, Thor pinned down the man with the scar and unleashed a flurry of fists upon him. The man gasped for air, taking in nothing but blood and broken bone. He lifted his arms in a vain attempt to defend himself before they came crashing down as his breathing ceased.

Loki pulled Thor to his feet.

CHAPTER TWO

THE ENDLESS CHASM of smoke and flame haunted Baldr. A terror crawling upon his very being, a vision of what would one day come to pass. And through the infinite lit blackness lay a lone sign of life: a mistletoe bush.

Baldr rose from his slumber in a sweat, craving something, anything, that would remove the world from around him. As he did every morning, he lumbered toward the water pot, washed his face, and regretted waking just as he regretted sleep. The bed was empty. Nanna had long abandoned it, unable to cope with her husband's nightmares. For three years they'd plagued him, though he knew not why. His life was not one of strife and struggle, but one of comfort. Baldr had long suspected that meaninglessness—*no great cause, no great mission, nothing but this feeble shelter*—was the cause.

It was still dark outside, no longer night but not quite morning. He made for the castle's dining hall. Upon entering the hall, most would find more food than a town would know what to do with, but it was much too early for that. The tables that stretched yards on end lay barren, not yet covered in their usual red cloth, revealing the cracked, unfinished wood beneath. A server approached Baldr as he sat.

"What would you like to eat, sir?" the server asked before naming the foods they had prepared for the degmal, the morning meal: lamb stew, grilled beef, pork, mutton, chicken, duck, and horsemeat (a delicacy only served once a week, perhaps twice if supplies allowed); local fruits as well as those imported from Midgard; and, of course, buttermilk.

"Mead," Baldr growled.

"And nothing to eat, sir?"

"Mead and more mead. The moment my tankard is empty, I expect to see another full to the brim."

The server obliged to Baldr's request, recalling that the prince had once had a hearty appetite, although not one that rivaled his brother's. Despite his gaunt appearance and the ever-present black circles underneath his eyes, Baldr remained the most handsome man in the land. He had long brown hair which curled around his shoulders and piercing green eyes. Unlike his father and brother, Baldr preferred to remain cleanly shaven.

In his younger years, he would escape the castle, only to return in the middle of the night with a girl on each arm. Marriage did not temper his love of women, nor women's love of him. Instead, with only a few exceptions throughout the years, he ensured that his extramarital trysts remained secret.

Try as he might, the world remained no matter how much he drank. And as his nightmares worsened, his drinking had evolved into an all-day affair. *They did this to me*, he thought as he slammed the fourth tankard on the table. Drink did not affect him as it once did, and he cursed his own body. *All I am is what they made me.*

Seeing what she perceived as Odin's roughness with Thor, Frigg, Baldr's mother and Odin's second wife, made Odin promise that he would not harm a hair on Baldr's head. The love of a mother can forge the strongest of men, yet, if unchecked, it can also breed coddled men, far too weak to ever leap from the nest. Baldr was the latter, a boy in men's clothing.

Without purpose, men fall adrift, floating through the vastness of their meaninglessness, cursing the very comforts that forged them, and cursing themselves as they continue to seek them out.

Baldr called out for another drink. No one answered. *Disrespectful curs.* He stood up to see the hall empty. Though he drank to escape the world, Baldr became oblivious to the fact that he had long since escaped it. It was the world in his mind that he yearned to run from. The constant nagging in his head, driving him to a path he had yet to see.

In all his years, Baldr could not recall ever seeing the hall empty. Through the fire of drunkenness and rage, he came to a sudden realization: *Something's wrong.* He made for the kitchen. Folded sheets of red silk lay on one side, and all around him were the carcasses of chickens, goats, and cows, some skinned, some cooked, and some left as they were, though dead, looking somewhat alive. He'd never seen the kitchen empty. *Where is everybody?* He closed his eyes, steadied his breath, and heard what he would have heard long ago had he not been drunk. The commotion was coming from outside.

The walls around him began to spin as he ran. Nevertheless, he kept moving. "Get him inside," called a voice in the distance. A crowd had formed around the castle entrance, men and women standing in shock at what they were seeing. Baldr pushed through only to see Thor hanging on Loki's shoulder, his eyes bloodshot red, his skin tinged with a mixture of purple and green, sweat coating every inch of him. *What has the Jotunn done?* Baldr thought as he placed his brother's arm around himself.

"Careful," Loki said, motioning his head toward the bandage wrapped around Thor's upper thigh.

The drunken haze vanished. "What happened?"

Thor mumbled something incoherent.

Loki remained silent.

"What happened?" Baldr asked once more. Loki said nothing, using what little strength he had left to lift the load bearing down on him. "Speak, Jotunn!"

"No time," Loki said in a voice that was barely a whisper. "We have to get him to Eir."

Baldr subdued the urge to leap at the Jotunn.

CHAPTER THREE

"A DECLARATION OF WAR!" Odin said. His voice reverberated throughout the room.

Odin was not what we would call in modern times a morning person, preferring to wake, at the earliest, two or three hours before noon. On most days, he would awake to a kiss on the forehead delivered by the lovely Frigg, his wife. If his mood so inclined, which it often did, Odin would begin his day with coitus. Then came a hefty degmal of grilled mutton or, depending on the season, salmon washed down with a large tankard of buttermilk. It was only after such pleasantries that his thoughts turned toward the craft of statesmanship.

At precisely two hours after noon, he would make for the counsel chamber. The chamber, located in the far wings of the castle, away from curious eyes and ears, was a large circular room. Books lined its walls end to end, most of which no one but Mimir had any interest in reading. A large oblong wooden table sat at the center of the room. As was the custom, the king sat at one end and his counsel at the other. Between them would sit anyone whom Mimir sought to invite to help facilitate the day's particular topic(s) of discussion.

That morning, rather than a gentle kiss on the forehead, Odin awoke to a loud and constant banging on his bedroom door. "What is it?" grumbled the king as he stumbled out of bed. "What is it?!" No answer came, and the knocking continued. He flung the door open. On the other side was Mimir, a palpable look of dread painted on his pale complexion.

"The prince," Mimir said.

"Thor?"

"We need you in the chamber immediately."

"Where's Thor?" Odin said as he entered the room, seeing only Loki and Baldr in front of him.

"You'd better sit down for this," Mimir said, leading Odin to his customary seat.

Loki took a deep breath before recounting the events that had transpired in Sirhilm. "It wasn't more than a flesh wound. Nevertheless, I managed to persuade him to come back here. On the third day, as Thor's condition began to worsen, I knew it was no ordinary blade. I checked the wound for infection but could find none. Without a doubt, the knife was poisoned."

Odin's eyes welled. His expression moved from weariness to rage. He made his proclamation, confident in no other explanation.

"We must not be too hasty," Mimir rebutted. "With the evidence presented, this appears to be nothing more than the actions of one man. Raining hell upon an entire nation for the actions of one bad actor is—" Mimir took a deep breath. "—ill-advised."

"What would you have me do?" Odin said. "Sit and do nothing while my son lays fighting for his life?"

"Nothing of the sort, sire. We must investigate this matter coldly and calmly. If this man was indeed a Jotunn assassin, we must find out posthaste. But if he was acting alone, retribution has already been delivered. Painfully, might I add, based on what Loki was saying. What is more curious to me is both why and how a Jotunn managed to venture so far south."

"Curious, isn't it," Baldr interjected. "A lone Jotunn finds himself in the exact same place as Thor while he's with Loki." Turning toward Odin, he said, "Do you think it is wise, Father, that we sit here and discuss the fate of Jotunheim while the true heir to Jotunheim's throne sits between us?"

"Leave," Odin whispered. The room fell silent. The silence was only broken by the squeal of Loki's chair. "Not you," Odin said, his voice firm but not loud. He turned and locked eyes with Baldr.

"As you wish, Father."

"Might I interject, sire?" Loki said. "Events such as this have a way of bringing up thoughts and emotions that often get the better of us. Baldr's words are those of a loving brother's frustration and grief, not to be taken personally. I prefer he stay and find comfort in our course of action."

Odin provided a wordless nod of approval before turning toward Mimir. "What do the whispers speak of Jotunheim?"

"The raids on Midgard grow more violent and are occurring more regularly. This is to be anticipated as winters grow harsher. Nevertheless, the Jotunns' attacks appear uncoordinated. A few tribes have unified, out of necessity rather than any higher ideal. As far as I'm aware, none have been so brazen as to enter our lands—until now, that is—but we must remember, without any trading partners, it wouldn't be unexpected for the Jotunns to act more brazenly."

Odin furrowed his brow. "And none have declared themselves?"

"Not as far as I'm aware."

"Tell me, Mimir, how much trust are we to place in these whispers?"

Mimir sighed. "I trust their loyalty to gold, sire."

"Which is to say, you do not trust them."

Gold is a strange metal. It was far too weak to be of any practical use to the inhabitants of Yggdra, yet, in an odd turn of events, gold's uselessness became its most valuable feature. In ages past, the peoples of Yggdra traded with wheat and barley. Trading in wheat and barley poses one fatal problem: They go bad. An economy based on a currency that is prone to rot is not what we would call today sustainable. Gold, which was scarce but not too scarce, proved to be an ideal alternative. Weapons, or for that matter anything of value the peoples of Yggdra made, couldn't be forged from gold. It was far too soft. No sane man would consider a useless metal valuable unless everyone else agrees to imagine that the metal is valuable. It remains a mystery which of the nine realms began trading with gold first. Nevertheless, the rest followed suit within a generation. As soon as people became united in their belief that the useless metal held value, people began to ornament themselves with it.

Knowing gold's value was entirely imaginary, a fiction people took as gospel, Mimir came to the belief that any loyalty bought with gold was, in turn, also imaginary. "Gold buys loyalty," for years he would tell Odin, "but loyalty bought with fiction is in itself nothing more than fiction." Odin had long taken these words to heart. Although he was not above buying men's loyalty, he made sure to regard any news or advice provided by such individuals as suspect.

"To find comfort in our knowledge," Mimir said, "I see only one course of action. By all admissions, it is a dangerous idea—one that, if pursued, would need to be handled with the utmost delicacy. I would have a party of our most trusted men enter Jotunheim and gather the information we seek."

"A dangerous course of affairs," said Odin.

"Indeed," said Loki. "As far as I'm aware, an Aesir hasn't set foot in Jotunheim in over twenty years. I can't envision a band of Aesir soldiers meandering through Jotunheim being too constructive to our cause. Can any of you envision anyone divulging any information to them? Moreover, it isn't beyond comprehension that whoever we send would be cut down the minute they entered Jotunheim. Seeing as Aesir blood cannot be left unavenged, such an event would no doubt result in war, something I assume all of us wish to avoid. Jotunheim being leaderless also presents us with a further complication, because if we do indeed follow through with Mimir's suggestion, and it does lead to war, we are left fighting a nation with no leader whom we might negotiate peace with."

"Then what would you have us do?" Mimir said calmly.

Loki shook his head. "I don't know."

"It seems war remains a distinct possibility, whatever course of action is taken," Odin said. "As such, we must prepare for it."

A shockwave made its way through Loki's being. "I don't think we're in any shape to make such a call."

"And why is that?" Baldr said.

"Jotunheim is leaderless. An ununified Jotunheim poses no military threat to us. If we prepare for war, we will accomplish nothing but readying ourselves for a quagmire with no exit."

"An attempt was just made on the heir to Asgard's throne," Baldr retorted. "Any information we do have on the comings and goings of Jotunheim is suspect. Can you really assert that Jotunheim is leaderless?"

Loki's face curled in frustration. "Such news that someone has claimed the throne of Jotunheim would undoubtedly reverberate throughout the nine realms."

"Brother," Odin said, "though I value your guidance, I must remind you that although you were born of war, you have never tasted it, and I pray you never will. If there remains a possibility, no matter how small, that enemies are conspiring to bring our downfall, we must be ready for it."

Mimir rubbed his hands together. "Sire, any news that Asgard is preparing itself for war will undoubtedly resonate throughout the nine realms. Do we expect the Vanir to take such news positively? Whether we intend it or not, if we ready our troops for war, we are inviting violence—the same violence your father spent his life trying to do away with."

"I do not wish to invite violence, my counsel, but I will not stand aside while the possibility of it looms over my head. Baldr, for too long comfort has burdened you. No more. In Thor's absence, I appoint you as Asgard's Master of Arms."

Unrequited love is a terrible burden to bear. But to be married to someone who does not love you is a burden altogether unholy.

Sigyn was, or at least appeared to be, the perfect woman. She had long golden hair that draped down and curled about her shoulders, brown eyes that held within them a slight hue of blue, pale skin, and a slightly crooked nose, an imperfection that only enhanced her beauty. Intelligent, kind, and a good mother, she should've been the perfect wife. Nonetheless, Loki could never find it in his heart to love her, or at least love her as much as he should have done, a fact he tried his best to hide but suspected his wife knew.

It was what she symbolized. A reminder that, no matter what he told himself, he remained a prisoner. A boy locked in a castle. "Love is the death of loyalty." Odin had hoped that, by marrying Loki to Sigyn, he would undo any remaining loyalty Loki held toward Jotunheim.

She was a handmaiden's daughter. As a girl, she would stare at the boy she would one day marry, playing out fantasies in her head. He wasn't like the other boys. Never too loud, brash, and, perhaps most importantly, rude. He was kind, soft-spoken, but never one to be gotten the better of. A bit of a practical joker, yes, but one with finesse. They didn't say a word to each other growing up. That made it all the more surprising when Mimir, whom Odin had tasked with finding Loki a suitable wife, approached her.

She soon found herself in a lineup of potential suitors (these were different times than our own). The boy she'd grown up admiring from afar had a sullen and slightly bored look on his face. He'd grown up to be a fine man. Handsome, gentle, counsel to the heir. As she stood there, shoulder to shoulder with over a dozen or so potential suitors, her heart leaped when he looked up at her and halfheartedly said, "I'll take the pretty one."

They were married within a fortnight, and she was pregnant not long after that.

Unlike other members of the Aesir elite, Loki did not think it honorable or decent to visit brothels during his wife's pregnancy. Sigyn was glad that, while her husband wasn't as warm with her as she would've liked, he maintained such a high sense of honor.

While most fathers were content to leave the raising of their children to their wives, Loki wasn't most fathers. A night when Nari did not fall asleep to his father's voice was a rare event. Under his father's tutelage, the boy could read by four and write (though not well) by five.

As Sigyn slept, Loki would often find himself staring at her. *I don't deserve you*, he'd think, as Odin's words, "Love is the death of loyalty," ran through his mind. Every night he told himself he would be a better husband, and every day she became a symbol of what he was and what he was not.

Something happened during Loki's six-month trip which he did not expect. He missed her. As he lay his head on the cold damp soil, he dreamed of her and her embrace. One night, looking at the stars, Thor's snoring covering the sound of crickets, he made a solemn vow to love her as she deserved, but given the circumstances, it was a promise he knew he could not now keep.

"I was so worried," Sigyn said, draping her arms around him. He closed his eyes, taking in her warmth, before kissing her on the head.

"Where's Nari?" he asked.

"Outside, playing. I thought we needed some time to ourselves."

He placed his head by her bosom and said, "I missed you." He meant every word.

"I missed you too."

Loki pulled down her silken gown and kissed her shoulder, then pulled himself back and, for a moment, stared into her eyes.

"What is it?" she whispered.

"Nothing. I just wanted to look at you," Loki said, believing it would be the last night he'd spend with her.

CHAPTER FOUR

MIMIR HAD LONG MADE it a habit to wake up before the break of dawn. It wasn't the quiet of the morning—those beautiful hours when all were asleep, and he could find time away from the rattling of gossip to think in peace—that motivated him. It was the view. As the realms lay in their beds, the sun made its display, showering the horizon in orange and yellow. The colors draped themselves atop the forest, which lay some two miles away from the castle, as the purple hue of not-yet-morning pranced atop the great mountain.

Standing outside one of the castle's many balconies, he found his thoughts wandering toward the events of the previous day. He had often found it helpful to allow his mind to roam, and rather than engage with these thoughts, found it soothing to observe them as if they were leaves drifting down a roaring river.

"Quite a performance you put on," Mimir said as the creak of the door behind him interrupted his thoughtless thinking. "Destiny can be described as fickle," he mused as Loki shuffled toward the bench to sit next to him, "although sometimes she's better described as a cruel bitch with a terrible sense of humor. If it is my blessing you seek, know that, as king's counsel, I cannot grant it, but I can't say I disapprove."

"How did you know?" Loki said.

"Because if I were you, I'd be thinking the same thing." Loki remained silent as his teacher spoke. "Destiny has claimed you, Laufeyson. You might try to escape her taloned clutches, but she has set her sights upon you."

"It is my choice."

"Aye, it is," Mimir said, "but what is destiny but the road between what we choose and what we don't. You made your choice as you dragged Thor back here. The way I see it, this conversation is merely a formality."

"Hardly a conversation when you're doing all the talking."

Mimir laughed. "A one-sided conversation is still a conversation." He took a deep breath and paused for a moment. "How far are you willing to go?" He put a hand on Loki's lap. "No, no, don't tell me. The less I know, the better. Situations such as this are fluid, malleable. Decisions will have to be made as events reveal themselves. Odin is none the wiser. Although I can't imagine he'll be best pleased with your sudden disappearance."

"I'm betting on his oath."

"A wise bet. Odin is not a man I would call honest. To him, pacts and promises are nothing more than suggestions. But this one oath, one made to a dying father, is one I cannot foresee him breaking."

"And what if he does?"

"Then all will be lost. You'll be dead, and I not long before or after. Jotunheim will burn and thousands, possibly tens of thousands, along with it. But there was one truthful statement said yesterday. No matter the choices we make, all roads in front of us point toward war. Your plan, if I deduced it correctly, remains our best hope for peace."

"He'll question you."

"And I will tell him exactly what you have told me of your plans, which is to say, nothing." Mimir leaned back and smiled. "Before you go, perhaps you might provide me with some insight into a question I have not found a satisfactory answer to. Some nights ago, on the outskirts of the forest, the ground opened up and swallowed three rangers whole."

29

"Excuse me?" Loki said, perplexed.

"Yes, you heard me right. A party of seven rangers ventured from the castle. Three disappeared. The surviving four claimed the earth beneath them shook, then opened up and swallowed their three comrades. My mind first went toward some sort of mutiny; their commanding officer was among those swallowed. However, it became apparent to me, due to their injuries, which were most assuredly not the result of combat, and my visit to the site of said event, that they were, in fact, telling the truth, or at least what they believe is the truth. What sort of phenomenon might cause the ground itself to open?"

Loki scratched his thin beard and stared at the horizon. "I have no clue what could've caused that."

"Then perhaps we can investigate this matter more closely upon your return."

A dull pain emanated from the pit of Loki's stomach as he realized —not knew but truly realized—this was possibly the last time he would ever speak to his teacher. "Thank you," Loki said, his eyes red but without tears, "for everything."

Mimir pulled his young apprentice close, hugging him as fiercely as he had ever done. "The honor was mine."

The medical bay had a faint chemical aroma, the result of Eir's tireless (and often fruitless) experimentation, to which Loki was not particularly partial as it tended to dry his eyes out and produce an irksome itching sensation in the back of his throat.

"He's much better today," Eir said, her voice a high-pitched squeal, a cross between a bird chirping and a squirrel chattering. "Not much I can do. Don't know what they got him with. We're just keeping him comfortable. He says he feels cold, but he's sweating like a pig. Terrible stuff they stuck him with. I wouldn't be opposed to getting my hands on some of the stuff, for research purposes, of course. If it were a lesser man, we'd all be saying our goodbyes right about now, probably even worse than that. But he's a strong chap. He'll be alright.

Sooner than most would think, too. If I didn't know him better, I'd have let him go today. But knowing him as I do, I'd say he's going to need another two or three days here. Just to be safe. No complaints from me on that front. Most of those who get sent here aren't as nice to look at. The open wounds and the constant screams of 'kill me, kill me,' make them even more unflattering—not that they were very flattering to begin with."

"Right," Loki said, processing the earful. "Do you think I'd be able to see him?"

"Definitely," she squawked. "He was speaking all sorts of gibble-gabble yesterday morning, called Sif a yellow aubergine with legs. Not something you say to your wife. Especially after not seeing her for six months. Goes without saying she didn't take it all too well. You can't blame him for speaking so improperly. He's been poisoned with who knows what. Got more lucid at around sundown. Couldn't remember calling her that. He was sweet then, calling her 'light of my eye,' 'prettiest in the realms,' and other things of a more explicit nature that no doubt flattered her but do not bear repeating in polite conversation. I gave them their privacy, and let's just say this: If more men had the, let's call it strength, of Thor on his bad days the world would be a much happier place. Needless to say, Sif left with the broadest smile on her face. Oh, the noises I heard."

Loki had heard too much, far too much. "Can I please see him?"

"Right this way," Eir said, guiding him through the winding corridors of the medical bay to the large room where Thor was located, speaking without pause all the way. (Loki made sure to remain quiet the entire time, mentally blocking out everything she prattled on about.) Although Eir's voice wasn't loud, it was piercing. Piercing enough to wake up Thor, who had only managed to fall asleep minutes prior.

"Spare the poor man," Thor said, rubbing away whatever sleep Eir's voice hadn't eviscerated from his eyes. Eir made a sound similar to a bird being shot and left, closing the door behind herself.

"You look good," Loki said, pushing the chair toward the bed. "Too bad there's nothing we can do about that ginger hair of yours."

"Funny," Thor grunted. "Don't say it."

"If only you'd listened to me—"

"Here we go."

"—you wouldn't be here."

"I just went through a near-death experience. I could do without you giving the 'I told you so' speech."

"But I did tell you so."

"That you did, you smug little bast—" He paused. "You know what, you just saved my life, so as much as it pains me to say it, thank you."

"What was that? I couldn't quite hear you."

"Thank. You."

"For what?"

"Don't milk it." Thor leaned back in the bed and smiled, recalling the last time he'd had occasion to visit the medical bay.

During his early teenage years, long before he was heir's counsel and such behavior was deemed improper, Loki had been partial to the occasional practical joke. Thor had long judged Loki as a bookish bore, an ever-present fixture by Mimir's side. His opinion shifted when he discovered Loki was behind what came to be referred to throughout the castle as 'the goat incident.'

Someone (Loki) thought it would be a wondrous idea to release four mountain goats into the castle. To make matters worse, on the side of every goat was a number painted in pitch. Goats one, two, three, and five were found on the same day. A search party, which Thor had the unfortunate honor of being part of, spent the better part of two weeks searching for goat number four.

Eir, worried the goat would come marauding into her chemical lab, made sure Thor checked every nook and cranny of the medical bay. She then made sure he stood on guard, hammer in hand, ready to face the beast if it made its nonexistent presence known.

The jig was up when a cleaner found a poorly stashed container of pitch in Loki's room. Much to everyone's chagrin, Odin did not chide Loki. The following day, as Loki made his way to Mimir's chamber, he found himself face-to-face with Thor, who was holding a wooden sword in his hand. "Do you know how to fight?" Thor said as Loki let out a large gulp. "I thought not. Everyone should know how to fight." He handed Loki the sword, smiled, and said, "You're not as boring as I thought you were." Loki was a terrible student. Try as he might, it would be years until Loki resembled anything close to a decent swordsman. But with a bow he had no equal, becoming a more able archer than even Thor.

Thor's eyes drifted toward Loki's clothing: a tattered shirt and mud-stained trousers. "You're leaving?"

Loki nodded. "Odin has given Baldr command of Asgard's armies. He is to ready them for war in your absence."

"War with who?" Thor said, trying his best to mask the oncoming smile.

"Jotunheim," Loki said. "Odin believes that the attempt on your life might be the result of some kind of conspiracy to bring down the throne of Asgard."

"He was one man, acting alone, and I killed him."

"I know. But Odin needs proof."

"Proof of what?"

"That no one has claimed Jotunheim's throne."

"And you're going to Jotunheim to find proof?"

Loki nodded.

Thor's expression softened. The smile crawled out of its hole and spread itself across Thor's lips.

"You knew?" Loki said.

"Of course I bloody knew."

"How?"

"Baldr being named Master of Arms, that's not something that stays quiet for very long. And Eir, by the gods, that woman can talk. I probably know more about what's going on in this castle than even Mimir. But most of all, I know you. Try as you might, you just can't help it. You see something wrong, some part of you just needs to get involved. I know how you think. It's quite obvious, really. Odin would never agree to it, but a Jotunn loyal to Asgard, you're the only one that can get whatever evidence Odin is looking for. Plus, those dirty rags you've got on are a dead giveaway." His smile disappeared, replaced with a solemn expression. "It's a dangerous road. And if you do make it back, Odin might not even trust you. Unless. . . ." He scratched his beard. "Unless your journey was at the command of the Master of Arms. The *real* Master of Arms, that is. Your mission is by my order." He looked down at the floor. "The path you're about to walk . . . there's no guarantee you'll make it back."

"I know," Loki said. "But if there's a chance I can stop a war from happening, it'll be worth it."

Thor placed his head in his palm. "Have I ever spoken to you about my mother?"

"No."

"But you know who she was, what she was?"

"I do."

"Queen Jord of Asgard and Jotunheim. Odin killed her when I was a baby. He doesn't think I can remember her, but I do. Her warm hands lifting me, cradling me, her smile, her brown eyes, her voice, her jet-black hair. I remember everything about my mother. She sang to me. Every night I fell asleep to her voice, her delicate voice and songs of faraway lands where the snow fell so thick it swallowed men whole.

"I was three when Odin slit her throat. She was not chosen for him. No, he loved her. They say the moment Odin saw fair Jord, nothing more than a maiden in Farbauti's halls, he swore by the sun and moon that he would take her as his wife. Despite that love—that burning love that I know, though he will never admit it, will never die out—he killed her. Why? Was it for some crime? No, he killed her because she was a Jotunn. Nothing more, nothing less.

"The path you are about to embark upon, it is not one of forgiveness and honor. It is one of vengeance and blood. Loki, it may have been Borr's mercy that spared your life all those years ago, but it was Odin's cruelty that kept you locked up like a criminal for twelve years. Odin only ever took you as a brother to fulfill his father's dying wish. I love my father, Loki, but I know what he is. Know this: Odin is not the only one in these halls with whom you share blood. You are my brother just as much as you are his."

34

Loki stood at the gate and closed his eyes. The smell of freshly cut grass filled the air. Even outside, the comings and goings, the hustle and bustle of the castle could still be heard. He took a moment to listen to it. To really listen to it. To take it in.

He looked to his left, then his right. No one was looking. Part of him hoped that as he set one foot in front of the other, a voice would call out to him. It might tell him that the path was too dangerous, that he was too valuable to place himself in such peril. Nothing came. As he walked, the voices faded faster than he expected. Then, there was nothing but the sound of the wind.

CHAPTER FIVE

BEYOND THE CASTLE LAY A FOREST, and beyond the forest lay a hill, and on the hill was the Tower. Legend has it the Tower reached the sky, allowing those inside to see the entirety of the nine realms. But legends have the propensity to exaggerate.

The Tower of Sight was no taller than a modern-day five-story building. The Watcher was given the unfortunate task of spending his life in the Tower and, as his name suggests, keeping watch. Watchers often began their careers with enthusiasm. Within mere months, that enthusiasm would vanish as they realized, firstly, that the Tower was far too short to see anything much of interest, and secondly, that if indeed the Watcher did manage to see an invading army making its way to the castle he'd have a hell of a job on his hands running back to the castle (it was deemed fiscally irresponsible to give the Watcher a horse), and thirdly, he had to spend most of his life doing nothing much at all. It was an honor, no doubt. But it was also an honor one wouldn't wish on their worst enemy. They'd found the previous Watcher hanging from a rope. The condition of the body led one to believe he'd been dead for some time.

The honor of Watcher had been Heimdall's now for just over three years. He took on the role with the same enthusiasm as a bored house cat, spending most of his time with his pants down and his manhood in hand. Once a month, food was delivered from the castle. He always relished food delivery days, but not because of the food. He was just glad to see another human being. The key point here being *see*, not *speak to*. A Watcher was to keep watch for as long as his eyes permitted him, meaning that when whoever had the unfortunate pleasure of delivering the food arrived and dropped the food by the door, the Watcher had better be keeping watch. Otherwise, he'd find himself keeping watch over three walls and some steel bars.

It was an hour before midday when Heimdall shot up out of bed, awoken by a voice saying, "Heimdall, you lazy prick, get out here and open the door." He pulled his pants up and opened the door.

"Loki, I didn't see you."

"Bad choice of words."

"What brings you here?"

"Oh, you know, checking our defenses, which of course begin with the Guardian of Asgard. The realm·owes you a great debt. Why, if it weren't for you, Asgard could be invaded in the night, and we would all be killed in our sleep. Knowing the mighty Watcher keeps watch makes me feel warm, safe, and secure."

Heimdall rolled his eyes. "What do you want?"

"Aren't you going to let me in?"

Heimdall grunted. The door squealed as he opened it. There wasn't much inside. A small bed, better suited for a child than a full-grown man; a small wooden chair, the sort of chair that encouraged one to keep on standing; the stairs; a wooden door to the basement; a small window; and nothing else but stone walls and mold.

Loki spread himself on the bed. "I have to say, once you get used to the smell, this place can be somewhat livable."

"What do you want?" said Heimdall, enunciating every word in a monotone.

"What if I was to tell you Odin has a mission for you."

"I'd say you're a trickster who kept me looking for a goat for two weeks, put crickets in my room, convinced me I had a shot with Sif while Thor was courting her—" He saw Loki wince, recalling the beating Thor had given Heimdall. "—and put tar in my socks."

"Fun times," said Loki. "Take solace in the fact that whatever I might have done to you doesn't compare to what you did to yourself by taking this job. If I'm not mistaken, there's supposed to be a tree outside," Loki pointed outside the window, "right about there."

"Needed firewood last winter."

"So you cut down the World Tree? That tree is four hundred years old. It is the symbol of the Watchers, firmly rooted, always in place, and you cut it down for some firewood?"

"No one told me! I didn't know what that tree was. Anyhow, how do you expect me to go get firewood and keep watch?"

Loki scratched his forehead. "Like every other Watcher before you. 'As far as his eyes permit' doesn't necessarily mean every second. Walk to the forest, you blasted imbecile." He sighed. "No, no, maybe Odin shouldn't have chosen you for this mission. It's far too risky."

"I am the Watcher. How am I supposed to keep watch if I'm off on some mission?"

"Who said the mission requires you to leave your post?"

"It doesn't?" asked Heimdall.

"Well, of course, it does," said Loki, "but you shouldn't have assumed so. Don't worry your little mind about it; a temporary replacement will be here before nightfall."

"This isn't some trick?"

"Are you questioning our king's orders?" said Loki with a smile.

Heimdall shook his head.

"Good," said Loki as he stood. "I'll have you know those days are long behind me."

"So, what is it? This mission. What am I meant to do?"

"You're going to take me to Jotunheim."

Heimdall's body stiffened. "No, no, I'm not. I knew it. This was a trick. I'll be damned before I go down as the Watcher who handed Jotunheim its king back."

"Fine," said Loki, "have it your way. You're more than free to go to the castle and ask Odin yourself, but I can't see him looking too kindly on someone questioning his orders."

"Why me?" said Heimdall, scratching his eyebrows.

"This is a mission that requires the utmost secrecy. The fate of Asgard hangs in the balance." Loki took a deep breath for dramatic effect. "A Jotunn assassin has made an attempt on Thor's life."

Heimdall let out a gasp, not unlike those seen in modern-day soap operas.

"Shocking, I know," said Loki. "A matter of trouble to the crown is whether the assassin was working alone, or whether the attempt was part of something larger and more sinister. If an Aesir were to walk into Jotunheim to investigate the matter, they would soon be found out and, in turn, killed. As I'm sure you know, Aesir blood cannot go unavenged. This would, in turn, force us into war with Jotunheim, something our king wishes to avoid if possible. As a Jotunn myself, I could walk through Jotunheim and no one would be the wiser. The king, in his infinite wisdom, has decreed that I make the trek and get to the bottom of this."

"And what is my part in all this?"

"No one knows the paths into Jotunheim as well as you, Heimdall. After all, wasn't it you that escorted Vycinder and Kyirin from Jotunheim undetected to train Thor all those years ago?"

"We'll go by water then; that'll be our fastest route."

The Little Sea, also called the Iving, was not a sea at all. It was a lake. Its area was so vast that it encompassed the borders of Asgard, Midgard, and Jotunheim. Given that most of Yggdra's inhabitants had never seen the sea, it is not difficult to understand why they called the Iving, the largest lake in the known world (or at least known at the time), a sea.

By water, the journey from Asgard to Jotunheim would've taken less than a day. In ages past, when the winters grew bitter and cold, the lake would freeze over completely, allowing fast travel between the two countries. It had been more than a century since winters had been so bitter.

Asgard's finest archers patrolled the Aesir portion of the lake, ready to make quick work of any who might be tempted to invade Asgard by water. Not even a dinghy had crossed the Iving in over two decades.

"No, I'm afraid the Little Sea is not an option," said Loki, pacing back and forth, feigning deep thought. "The guardians are not aware of the situation, and, considering the sensitivity of the matter, Odin sees it fit to shroud this mission in as much secrecy as possible."

"Through Midgard—there is no other way."

"Agreed," Loki said.

"You're going to need something warmer than that," Heimdall said, motioning his head toward the clothes Loki was wearing. "No matter how cold you think Jotunheim is, it's colder. You're also going to need weapons. I hope we don't have to use them, but it's better to have them and not need them than to need them and not have them."

"Then, we'll have to procure some on our way."

"No need," said Heimdall. "The Tower is nothing if not well equipped. We have everything we need right here."

And with that, Heimdall opened the small wooden door, revealing a narrow but winding staircase. It was dusty, smelling of damp and shattered dreams, and was exactly what they needed. Over the generations, the Tower had claimed many Guardians. In what had slowly become an unwritten and uncelebrated tradition, the possessions of past Watchers remained in the Tower, in the basement, visited only by the bored.

In the cobweb-filled room, they found everything they needed. Among the clutter was a black coat that Loki took a liking to. Perhaps more important was the bow, no doubt a royal gift. It was old, though how old was impossible to tell. More than decades, that was for sure, as the wood used to build the bow was of a sort Loki had never seen before. It had a light orange hue. The craftsmanship was clearly the work of the ancient Aesir (the quality of the Aesir's craftsmen had deteriorated with time). The string was made of silk, so thin yet so strong Loki nearly cut his finger pulling on it. The arrows were far younger, although by no means youthful. The work of the smiths of Svartalfheim. The markings on the tips were a dead giveaway.

Similar carvings could be found on the blade they found, but this was a sword with many previous masters. While it may have been crafted in Svartalfheim, the hilt was without a doubt of Aesir crafts-manship, as were the many improvements and alterations done to it. Those who didn't know better might have even believed that the blade was completely of Aesir make. Compared to other swords, it was somewhat short. Loki had always found broadswords to be cumber-some. This was a far better fit.

As he walked up the stairs, coat swung on his back, weapons in hand, a wave of excitement took him. At that moment, all the troubles of the world seemed to vanish as a stark realization gripped him. He was going on an adventure.

CHAPTER SIX

THOR'S MORNING following Loki's visit had been, for the most part, pleasant. Eir saw to it that Thor received a hearty degmal of roast beef and potatoes. After all, a man of his size would need the energy for healing. The headache had mostly faded, rearing its ugly head only momentarily, then dissipating.

While the morning was pleasant, it was by no means fun. As expected, the castle had erupted into somewhat of an uproar following Loki's sudden disappearance, meaning those who would've visited Thor were now scouring every inch of the grounds, searching for someone who was already miles away, dragging the realm's Watcher off on a "mission" the Watcher would bloody well end up regretting.

At just after noon, bored, and with no one to speak to, Thor decided to take a nap. It was a fine nap. One in which the blackness of sleep cuddles you and dreams are nowhere to be seen. It was the sort of nap that lasted longer than anything called a nap had any right to be. Then, after the sun had set, a voice filled with irritation feigning strength woke Thor up.

"Where is he?" Baldr's face was stern, his arms crossed as he leaned over Thor's bed.

"Good to see you, brother," Thor said, wiping his eyes. "But I have to say I'm rather disappointed. Your big brother is nearly killed, and you don't have the decency to come and visit him, and when you do, you come in here all angry asking 'Where is he?' like I have any idea what in the world you're on about. Terrible manners. Maybe you would not have turned out like this had father let me kick your teeth in once in a while when we were children."

Baldr's expression remained still. "Where is he?" he repeated.

"Who?" said Thor. "Where's who? If you haven't noticed, I'm bedridden. So, if you'd be so kind as to present me with a little context to your question, I'd be most grateful."

"You know bloody well who."

"By the gods, brother, I don't."

Baldr slammed his fist down on the bedside table. "This is not the time for games, Thor. Tell me now."

Thor scrunched his face into a ball. "Did that hurt? It looks like it hurt. Maybe I should get Eir to look at your hand. Eir!"

"Where is Loki?"

"Oh, him. Why didn't you say him?"

"Where is he?"

"He's faster than you think over long distances. Believe it or not, I had a lot of trouble keeping up with him over our journey."

Baldr took a step back, his breathing growing sharper. "What have you done? Where is he?"

"I sent him to Jotunheim."

"You what?!"

"Sent him to Jotunheim to investigate the attempt on my life. If we send a merry band of Aesir up there, I don't think many people would be willing to divulge anything of interest to them. But, thankfully, we have a Jotunn, and not just any Jotunn, but the smartest man in the nine realms. As the Master of Arms, it is well within my powers to send such a man as Loki — father's brother, might I add — to investigate whether the attempt on my life is the action of one man or part of some larger Jotunn plan to bring Asgard to its knees. In any case, I firmly believe the incident was the work of one man, a man whom I killed by caving his head in with my bare fists. In my opinion, justice has been served. But you know Father — ever the dramatist, ready to overreact at the slightest sign of trouble. By sending Loki to investigate, we'll be able to know, beyond a shadow of a doubt, what the real story is."

Baldr's face contorted into several shapes in quick succession. "And who said you're the Master of Arms?"

"Yes, I heard about your *temporary* appointment. Quite odd, really. I was gone for six months, and Odin didn't see it fit to appoint a temporary master then, and now he chooses to appoint, out of all people, you." Thor let out a chuckle. "I can't imagine any preparations for a potential war with Jotunheim would go down smoothly with you in charge. In any case, sweet, innocent, simple Baldr, Father gave you command of Asgard's armies due to me being poisoned and bedridden. But as you can see, I heal faster than most, and I'll be more than capable of commanding our troops in no time. But don't worry, brother. When I'm king, I might, maybe, possibly, think of choosing you as my successor, so think of your temporary appointment as, if my judgment deteriorates with age, practice."

Baldr's left eye began to twitch. "Do you have any idea what you've done? You've handed the Jotunns their king."

"Are you questioning our father's brother's integrity?" Thor pushed himself upright on the bed. "You know, it's quite a clunky phrase, 'father's brother.' But it doesn't seem right to call him uncle, does it? Uncle Loki, imagine that."

Baldr leaned over the bed and grabbed Thor by the collar. "I should've known that you'd be sympathetic to the Jotunn cause . . . considering that Jotunn bitch mother of yours."

Suddenly, Baldr found himself on the other side of the room, gripping his chest, unable to breathe. Thor towered over him, intimidating even in a dressing gown. "Mention my mother or speak to me that way again, and I'll do to you what I did to that Jotunn in Sirhilm."

CHAPTER SEVEN

"Try to catch up," yelled Loki.

Heimdall gasped, stared up the hill, and thanked the sun and stars that he'd, for the first time in nearly two weeks, be able to fall asleep in a bed rather than a pile of leaves. *This used to be easier*, he thought as Loki, who hadn't had to spend the last three years stuck in a tower with limited exercise space, walked past him, waited for him to catch up, then walked past him again.

Midgard's grasslands were more beautiful than he'd remembered. Some years ago, Loki had visited Midgard, alongside Thor, hoping to gain a greater understanding of the realm's farming practices. In that regard, their trip was unsuccessful. Bembuldir, whose farm lay on the other side of the hill, was a gracious host, teaching Loki everything he knew. (Thor, they all agreed, was useless as a farmer.) Loki returned to Asgard only to find that, even though he replicated everything Bembuldir had taught him, nothing grew in Asgard quite like it did in Midgard. Yes, the tomatoes grew, but they were not as red, not as succulent. Yes, the potatoes grew, but not as large and not as starchy.

"This is a blessed land," Bembuldir would tell Loki. "I cannot take credit for this bounty. Well, at least not completely."

Loki looked forward to seeing Bembuldir once more, but more

than that, he looked forward to eating the apples the man grew, right off the tree. For some reason Loki wished he knew, fruit tasted best the moment it was picked off the tree. By the time it traveled to Asgard, it had lost something, some essence, and didn't quite taste the same. Nevertheless, Loki made sure the castle was always stocked with Bembuldir's apples.

"Slow down," yelped Heimdall, gasping for air.

"If you'd only hurry up, we'd get there before sundown."

Heimdall grunted, knowing Loki was right, and put one foot in front of the other. The sun lay an inch above the horizon, still high enough to paint the sky anything but blue, but not for long. The clouds above were white. A lone grey cloud swam with them. Unlike the rest, it swept down from the sky and onto the horizon.

"So what's your alias going to be?" Heimdall said as Loki slowed his pace.

"What?"

"Your alias, when you get to Jotunheim. I mean, you're not going to go around telling everyone, 'I am your rightful king,' now, are you. You're going to need an alias, a false identity, a story to tell when people ask you who you are."

Loki laughed. "Still working on one."

"So, what've you got?"

"Loki's a common name in Jotunheim, so I reckon I won't have to change my name. The occupation remains a mystery to me. Tell me, Heimdall, what do you think this fictional Loki's vocation should be? Perhaps hunting?"

Heimdall let out a small laugh. "A man of your size, a hunter, really?" Loki looked at him, puzzled and half insulted. "You're the smallest Jotunn I've ever seen. Ice fishing might be a more believable vocation. It's a craft that would be more suitable for a man of your build."

"Ice fishing," Loki mused, trying to pretend that Heimdall's comment didn't bother him. "An honest job, one that wouldn't draw much attention. I like it. 'Loki the fisherman' has a nice ring to it."

Ahead of them in the sky the lone dark cloud grew in size, covering the white of its neighbors. Heimdall scrutinized it, his body tightening as he realized the cloud wasn't, in fact, a cloud. A sudden jolt of energy coursed through his body, an energy he hadn't felt in years. Without a word, he quickened his pace. "No, no, no, no," he whispered as his pace turned into a full-on sprint.

They ran as fast as their legs could carry them, Loki stopping to ready his bow, Heimdall with sword in hand. The farm burned. Screams, though faint, emanated from the distance. The screams of a man, his wife, and his daughter.

On the other side of the hill, the grass was replaced by tall stalks of wheat. Loki's eyes darted back and forth, but Heimdall was too far ahead to be seen. He coughed through the smoke, keeping one eye open, bow in hand. The orange glow came from all around. He ran forward and back, left and right, seeing nothing but the stalks and the glow. Then came the scream—wordless, shrill, desperate. Loki sprinted toward it. Then came the voice. No, not a voice. Many voices. Laughing. Cawing. Cooing.

"My, my, you're a tasty one," said the man, towering over the girl. "Very tasty."

Those were the last words he spoke. An arrow pierced his eye socket before he could realize what was happening. He fell to his knees, reaching for the arrow, only to have another pierce his heart.

"Are you alright?" said Loki as the girl crawled backward. She pointed behind him, her mouth shaping a scream her throat couldn't produce. The club hit Loki on the back of the head. He rubbed his eyes and looked up, recognizing his assailant to be a Jotunn.

"Kin-killer," roared the Jotunn. "Your lot. Too stingy."

Loki rolled, dodging the next blow. He shot up and unsheathed his sword.

"Pretty blade," the Jotunn said. "I'm going to make you eat it."

Loki stepped back, providing himself with much-needed distance. The Jotunn swung the club. Loki ducked and lunged at the Jotunn's legs. Though the blade made contact, it was only a minor flesh wound. The Jotunn flung his fist at the back of Loki's head. He looked up, only to see his sword in the Jotunn's hands.

"Where did you get this?" said the Jotunn, his eyes on the blade, a look of dread painted on his face. "This is an Aesir sword. It can't be. No, no, no. Don't tell me you've been killing Aesir? You're a madman. Killing Aesir. Positively mad. What are you trying to get us into? Another war?!" The Jotunn leaped at Loki, the Aesir blade aimed at his stomach. Loki closed his eyes.

The clash of steel on steel reverberated through his ears.

Heimdall roared, pushing the Jotunn back, standing firmly in front of Loki. The Jotunn lunged, only to find his head several feet from his body.

CHAPTER EIGHT

THE FIRE DID NOT SUBSIDE until early the next morning, covering all in a mist of grey and black. Bembuldir's eyes were red, his lips quivering, holding the only woman he'd ever loved. The look of sheer terror on her frozen face, an encapsulated moment best forgotten, etched into eternity. Everything he had was gone. Fourteen years of marriage ended with a laugh and a slit throat.

That morning, he dug, taking no help. This was his burden and his alone. The sun brought with it a terrible vision. Charred hopes, lives, and livelihoods. As he stood above the grave, tears flowing from his eyes, his daughter, Shiara, awaited what he would say, but nothing came to him. What was there to say, anyway? She understood. What he felt, she felt. A faint tint on reality, a trick, a horrible dream without the comfort of waking. He wiped the tears from his eyes, gripped the shovel close, digging into the mound of dirt meant to cover the body lying beneath the white sheet.

Loki stepped forward to help only to find a hand on his shoulder, turning to see Heimdall shaking his head as if to say, wordlessly, "Let him have this. He needs this." Seven had fallen the previous evening, and only one of them would receive anything resembling an honorable departure. The bodies of the six Jotunns remained where they fell, hewn husks of meat left for the circling vultures above.

Shiara was barely fourteen. Seeing the grief in her eyes, Loki stumbled on a thought he half cursed himself for having. He was glad, or at least thankful, that he was too young to remember his parents. Their deaths weren't real to him. But to her, she'd seen it: she'd heard her mother's screams, the spray of blood as the blade cut her throat. He was happy—no, not happy, but something akin to it that language dare not express—that he didn't have to see it with his own parents.

After the burial, they sat in a circle, all four staring at the ground. It was Bembuldir that broke the silence. "She told me this would happen," he said, letting out a sigh. "That I should just let them be—let them take what they need and leave. But no, I had to be the bigger man. 'This is my land,' I told her, 'and I'll be damned long before someone steals from my land.' One day, I waited for them. They were going for the cattle. I shot one of them dead right then and there. A woman. It wasn't dignified. The vultures picked her clean. Nothing left. She told me they'd be back, but not for food this time. Recompense." A shiver went through his body. "I killed her as much as they did," said Bembuldir, motioning at the shallow grave not twenty feet away from them.

"You can't blame yourself," Loki said as the girl clung to him. "If only you'd sent word. Asgard would've protected you."

"We are not under the protection of your king, or any king, for that matter. We are a free people here in Midgard, and we will stand strong through all that comes with that freedom."

"What will you do?" said Heimdall.

Bembuldir shook his head. "I don't know."

"Take your daughter to Asgard, to the castle," said Loki.

"What did I just tell you? We are a free people."

"Freedom be gone, man. Think of her." Loki gripped the girl tightly. "We can help you. Provide you with supplies, money, anything you need to get yourself started again."

Bembuldir put his index finger to his mouth and closed his eyes. "And I would be free to do as I wish with what I grow?"

"You would."

"Can you promise me that?" asked the farmer.

"I can," Loki replied, turning to his companion. "Heimdall, escort the man and his daughter to the castle."

Heimdall shook his head in refusal.

Loki sighed, nodded in understanding, and pulled an arrow from his scabbard. "Take this," he said to Bembuldir. "When you get to the castle, present them with this. Ask for Thor. Speak to no one but Thor. Tell him what I have promised you; he will see to it that it be done."

Heimdall placed a hand on Loki's lap. "A moment," he said, motioning his head toward a clearing several feet away and just out of earshot.

Loki nodded and accompanied him.

"It's over," said Heimdall. "We have an answer."

Loki shot him an inquisitive look.

"You have three witnesses. Me, you, and the girl. You heard what the Jotunn said. When he thought you'd killed an Aesir and taken his sword, he was terrified. There is no plot to attack Asgard. Justice has been served here. We'll return with them to the castle and tell Odin what happened. The girl will corroborate what we say. There's no need to go to Jotunheim."

"It's too convenient."

Heimdall furrowed his brow and stroked his chin. "You haven't been sent by Odin, have you?"

"No," said Loki, his voice more husky than usual.

"You never wanted me to get you to Jotunheim. You brought me along to make sure that whoever you bring back from Jotunheim gets to the castle unharmed and undetected."

"You're smarter than you look, Heimdall. Yes, this is what you might call an unsanctioned mission. Odin has no idea where I am. He's preparing the army for war. Within a few days, the fields surrounding the castle will be teeming with soldiers. He says it's only a precaution, but if history tells us anything, preparations for war are often followed by an actual war, regardless of the original intent.

Odin's not going to believe us if we go back now. It's too convenient. He'll think that I've paid Bembuldir off to say whatever I want him to say. 'Gold buys loyalty, but loyalty bought with fiction is in itself nothing more than fiction,' remember? No, I need it to come from a Jotunn. How I'm going to convince one to follow me, I have not the foggiest clue. But if I manage to get him to you, you might, against all conceivable odds, manage to sneak us into the castle through the catacombs, undetected, before someone kills us. Then maybe, just maybe, we can convince Odin that Jotunheim is not a threat. If we fail, thousands, possibly tens of thousands of innocent men, women, and children are going to die needlessly."

"Jotunheim is not a very safe place. What if you don't make it back?" Heimdall asked.

Loki took a deep breath and closed his eyes. "The last thing Odin swore to his father was that he would never harm me. If I die in Jotunheim, and Odin doesn't know I'm dead, he won't attack it out of fear that his troops, under his orders, might kill me, not knowing who I am. If I die in Jotunheim, and Odin doesn't find out, we win. But if I die on the way back—" Loki took in a deep breath. "—it'll all be for nothing."

PART II
JOTUNHEIM

.

CHAPTER NINE

YGGDRA WAS MORE SPARSELY POPULATED than might be imagined. Jotunheim, the largest of the nine realms, had a total of nineteen towns and a population of just under two hundred thousand; before the last war, it was reputed to be home to more than half a million. Asgard was far smaller. It had five towns and a population of just under forty thousand. Midgard was sparser still, with three main market towns and a population just shy of fifteen thousand.

Located a mere two-day journey from the Jotunheim border, Fildred was the smallest of Midgard's market towns. It had once been the primary outpost for trade with Jotunheim. After the war, when trade with Jotunheim ceased, the town found its economy sustained by its inns, taverns, and brothels. People traveled to Fildred from all over to engage in what one might call pleasantries of a more explicit nature.

Three weeks of minimal rest and sleep took its toll on Loki. To compensate, Heimdall changed their journey's course to pass through the town.

Loki stared at the grime-coated mead tankard, pondering whether to take a sip or cast it aside. Heimdall, on the other hand, was four drinks in, eagerly asking the barman to recommend establishments catering to the supply of female companionship. He returned to the table, fifth drink in hand, smiling, his face red and sweating.

"I think I like this plan of yours," Heimdall said. They agreed Heimdall was to remain in Fildred while Loki ventured into Jotunheim. If Loki didn't return in six months, Heimdall would go back to his post.

"Try not to catch something that'll kill you while you wait," said Loki before moving the dirt-encrusted tankard to his lips. He slammed the still-full stein back down on the table. "How on earth do you drink this?"

"You spend long enough in that bloody tower, anything tastes like the nectar of the gods." Heimdall licked his lips. "We need to find somewhere to rest tonight. You've got a long road ahead of you." He let out something, not a cough nor a burp, but an amalgam of the two. "I know it's not what you usually do but, before facing the cold and near-certain death, it might be nice to have a pretty little thing warm your sheets."

Loki pushed the tankard away.

"Have it your way," Heimdall replied.

A rough and sizeable hand gripped Loki's shoulder. "You're not from around here, are you?" said the man. He was tall and broad, but with a hunched back. He was cross-eyed and his clothes were tattered, yet he wore four golden chains around his neck. "The name's Iroc." Loki outstretched his palm only to find his arm being shaken with such force his shoulder nearly popped out of its socket. "Not many friendly Jotunns left. Rare find. It's as if Borr killed the good ones, and all we're left with are the raid-and-pillage type." He moved closer to Loki. "You got a name, stranger?"

"Loki."

"Well, Loki, what do you do for a living?"

"Fisherman. And yourself?"

"You see this reputable establishment?"

Loki nodded.

"I built this place with my own two hands. Brought in stones from the mountain, laid them down stone by stone. Carved that bar over there, this table, and the chair you're sitting on. But do they call me Iroc the tavern builder? No. That stone wall you saw on the way into town, I built that faster than any other man could. But do they call me Iroc the wall builder? No. There's a pier, about a week away from here, on the Iving. Built it with my own two hands, drove them piles in deep and strong so that it'll last a hundred lifetimes. But do they call me Iroc the pier builder? No. But you fuck one goat. . . ."

Loki let out a small chuckle.

"You like jokes, do you, Loki of Jotunheim? Well then, let's hear one from you."

"A man is walking through the countryside when he spots a sign saying, 'Talking Horse for Sale.' He walks towards the horse and begins to think to himself, *What an exciting life this horse must've had if it is a talking horse.* He asks the beast, 'What have you done with your life?' The horse neighs, steps back, looks left then right, and says, 'I've had a full life. I was born in Midgard. When I was two, an Aesir bought me. I spent my youth fighting. After he died, they sold me to a teacher. I spent years teaching children to read and write. Not proud of the fighting, but the teaching, I'm proud of that. Then the teacher died, and I got sold to this schlub.' The horse points to its master with its tail. 'Why on earth would you want to sell such an amazing creature?' the man asks the master. 'Because he's a damned liar,' says the master. 'Everything he told you is bullshit.'"

Loki wiped his face from the damp residue of Iroc's belly laugh.

"You like horses, do you, Loki of Jotunheim?" Iroc said, a look of filth-laden glee on his face. "Well, you heard of Svadilfari, fastest horse in the nine realms?" Loki shook his head. "Taller than any horse you ever laid eyes on, stronger, faster. She's got a bit of an appetite, eats more than any horse I've seen. She could traverse the fields of Mydoc in less than a day, taking no rest, might I add. Finest steed the world has ever seen."

"I find that hard to believe," Heimdall interjected. "Having crossed the fields of Mydoc myself, I can tell you that no one would be able to make the journey in a day, much less half a day. A day and a half, maybe, but one day, bollocks."

"Is that so?" Iroc swirled his grease-soaked mustache. "Loki of Jotunheim, your friend here doesn't believe me. What if I was to tell you that, yes indeed, I, me, Iroc, the greatest builder in the nine realms, have crossed the fields of Mydoc in less than a day, for you see, Svadilfari is my horse."

"And where is this magnificent steed of yours?" said Loki.

"Why, she's here. Well, not *here* here—they don't let horses into respectable establishments, such as this. She's tied out back in the stables."

The color vanished from Heimdall's face upon seeing the smile forming on Loki's lips. A smile any wise man would do well to worry about.

Loki gently pushed his seat back. "Excuse me, gentlemen."

"You take your piss, Loki of Jotunheim. We'll be right here when you're done."

A few quiet moments passed before the neighing of the horse reverberated through the tavern. Iroc shot up in his seat and rushed toward the door. Heimdall keeled over, laughing.

Seeing his horse gallop away, Loki on its back, the only words Iroc managed to say were, "Get back here with my horse, you sheep-shagger!"

CHAPTER TEN

LOKI SINCERELY DOUBTED that Svadilfari was the fastest horse in the nine realms, but by Odin's beard, it was undoubtedly the quickest horse he'd ever ridden. All around him, trees transformed into blurred lines of green and brown. What would've taken him two or perhaps three days on foot would now, with the help of Svadilfari, take scantly half a day.

What shocked Loki, even more than the horse's sheer velocity, was how quickly the landscape around him changed. On the first day, the green grass below turned into thick mud. Still, Svadilfari trotted on, although not nearly as fast as she had the previous day. That night, as Loki lay in the cold and damp of the desolate borderlands, his thoughts turned to Sigyn.

For a week, Loki saw nothing but dirt. It was a dry land, one far too cold for anything to grow. As he and the horse moved forward, guided by nothing but the maps found in the Tower, the landscape around them changed once more. The cold froze the earth—soil as hard as ice, and black as night. The wind came two days later and the snow three days after that.

Ten days had passed since their last meal, and their only source of water was melted ice. The horse, at long last, grew slow. Loki had taken to walking it rather than riding it. Then came the first sign of life—a lone deer wandering through the white wilderness. Loki withdrew his bow, took careful aim, and filled his belly with deer meat that night. To his surprise, with nothing else to eat, Svadilfari nibbled on the uncooked carcass. If horses were capable of grimacing, Svadilfari would have certainly done so.

The way to Jotunheim was steep, far steeper than most horses could handle. Thankfully, Svadilfari wasn't most horses. Seemingly grateful for never having to endure Iroc's company ever again, the horse grew fond of its new master.

On an unusually cold and dark night, Loki stared at the map, hoping beyond hope that he was indeed where he thought he was. According to Heimdall's map, there would be a town called Melvitar not three days away, possibly less. His eyes drifted, fading to grey, and then there was nothing but black.

Then came the red.

Loki screamed as the spear pierced his back. Voices clamored in the darkness—one, two, three, four, five of them. The warm blood of the now headless horse rubbed his cheeks. Loki placed his palm on the earth and attempted to push himself up. There was no movement —nothing but blood and searing pain.

"That'll feed us for a month," said one of them, sinking his dagger into Svadilfari, skinning the flesh.

Loki's mouth twisted and turned, but nothing came out. The red began to fade to grey once more; then, once again, it turned to black, and in the background, swords clashed.

CHAPTER ELEVEN

LOKI AWOKE, half expecting to find himself in Valhalla, but instead finding himself alone in a clay hut, a small fire burning in the middle, and a bowl of what he assumed to be Svadilfari stew on the dining table. He rubbed his lower back, touching a bandage where the spear had pierced him. He pushed himself upright. The bed was a thin but tall thing and as comfortable as a bed of nails. A yell burst out of him as he attempted to stand, placing his hands on the railing for support. The wooden door creaked open.

"Hope you weren't too attached," said the woman as she entered, motioning her head toward the plate on the table.

"That was the fastest horse in the nine realms," said Loki with a wheeze.

"It was," replied the woman, taking a bite of the stew. "Now, it's dinner." She sat down on the table, facing the bed, resting her feet on a chair. "No honor stabbing a man in the back while he's sleeping." She passed Loki a plate.

"Thank you." Loki took a bite of his travel companion. His eyes darted to the corner of the room. There, four swords and an ax leaned against the wall.

"Those will fetch a pretty penny," said the woman. "Winters are growing colder. Need every penny you can get; then you have to hope that there's someone stupid enough to buy from you."

"What's your name?" said Loki.

"Angrboda."

"Lovely name."

She shot him a dirty look. "And you are?"

"Loki."

"And what brings you here, Loki?" said Angrboda.

"The Little Sea. I was hoping to get a catch before the winter. It gets rough out there during winter."

"So you're a fisherman?"

"I am."

Angrboda let out a small laugh. "Who are you, really?"

"What do you mean?"

"You know exactly what I mean." She moved toward the corner of the room. Near the propped-up swords and ax was a red-dyed sheet. "I'm curious to know how a Jotunn fisherman managed to get his hands on an Aesir bow and blade," she said as she revealed the weapons beneath the cloth. "Now, are you going to tell me who you are or not?"

"I told you the truth." Loki's body stiffened.

Angrboda grabbed an arrow from the quiver and traced her fingers around the head. "Where did you tell me you were from?"

"I didn't," said Loki, realizing he didn't have the strength to run.

"So, where are you from?"

"Melvitar."

Angrboda howled in laughter. "You aren't making this any easier for yourself. Now," she said, rubbing the bowstring between her thumb and index finger, "are you going to tell me who you are, or am I going to have to shoot you?" She drew the arrow, aiming it at Loki's head. "Five."

"I told you the truth."

"Four."

"Calm down. There's no need for this."

"Three."

"Put the bow down, please."

"Two."

"I told you who I am."

"One."

"I am Loki, son of Farbauti and Laufey, rightful heir to the throne of Jotunheim, and I demand you lower that weapon!"

Angrboda stepped back, letting out a dry gulp of air. She lowered the bow, a palpable look of shock and awe painted on her complexion. Her lips only managed one word. "Shit."

CHAPTER TWELVE

As ONE GUARD KEPT WATCH, the other slept. Behind them, on the field that had been empty only a few nights ago, was the Aesir army. For now, it was three hundred strong. Within a fortnight, it would grow to its full might of four thousand.

A lone figure, the guard noticed, made its way through the darkness. The guard dug his elbow into his partner's ribs. "Oi, wake up, you lug." The sleeping guard grunted, his eyes still shut. "Oi, wake up."

"Not my shift yet," mumbled the half-asleep guard.

"There's someone out there."

The half-asleep guard was no longer half asleep. He rubbed his eyes and coughed. "Where?"

"Right there," said the on-duty guard, pointing out into the distance.

The off-duty guard squinted. "That's not a someone. That's a someones."

"What?"

"There's two of them. Look, one big one and one little one."

"Oh yeah, you're right. What do ya reckon, it's the enemies scout?"

"Nah, no scout's dumb enough to come that close. Looks like one of them's a kid. Poor sod's probably just lost."

"What should we do? Should we tell anyone?"

"Nah. If it's a lost sod, we'll send him away in the right direction. If it's an enemy, well, I haven't seen action in a long time and don't mind getting a little warm-up."

They sat and waited as the two figures got closer. The man had long brown hair and a long wild beard; black circles lay under his eyes. He was well built. Not the build of a soldier; he was far too bulky. No, it was the build of a farmer. The little girl by his side had hair so long it reached her waist.

"Anything we can help you with?" said one of the guards.

"I'm here to see Thor," said Bembuldir, holding Shiara tightly by his side.

"Is that right?" said the other guard with a mild chuckle. "And you are?"

"The name is Bembuldir, friend to the Aesir crown, and this is my daughter, Shiara. We are here to speak to the prince and the prince alone. We request that no others be informed of our presence. It is a matter of the utmost urgency."

The two guards laughed in unison. "Who the bloody blazes do you think you are? Coming here, ordering us not to tell anyone and talking about 'utmost urgency.' I'd cut you down right here if it weren't for that wee little thing attached to your waist. Now, get out of here before we change our minds and gut you."

Bembuldir pulled out Loki's arrow. "I've come to meet Thor and Thor alone. Inform him of my name and give him this." He handed one of the guards the arrow. "Tell him I have news of the mission."

"What bloody mission? In case you haven't heard, Thor's busy."

"Wait," said the other guard, interrupting his partner, motioning his head toward the arrow. "This is of royal mark."

"You believe him?"

"Not sure. But we have to tell Thor. Looks like he might be telling the truth . . . and if he is, and we turn him away, you'd better bet there'd be repercussions for the both of us. Terrible repercussions." The guard shifted toward Bembuldir. "Wait right here. Don't move a muscle. And you—" He turned to his partner. "—keep an eye on them. I'll be back as fast as I can."

Bembuldir waited. The red that precedes dawn glazed the sky. No words were said, only the occasional grunt, sigh, or cough. Then, as morning came, the guard returned. "Follow me."

Bembuldir had always found the castle to be confusing. Hallways followed by corridors that all looked the same. Though he'd visited the castle multiple times before, he'd never ventured so deep inside.

Thor's living quarters were more rugged than one would've expected for a member of royalty. Wooden, barely finished, furniture without the delicate engravings others came to expect as mandatory. Grey walls of undecorated stone. More akin to the quarters of a soldier than a prince.

"Dear friend," said Thor, "what brings you here?"

"My farm," said Bembuldir, his lips half trembling, "it's gone. Limtra, my wife, she's gone too. They burned it down. If it weren't for Loki and Heimdall, we'd also be dead."

Thor listened intently as Bembuldir painted a clearer picture of what had happened that night on the farm. He then sat cross-legged on the floor, stroking his beard, staring at nothing in particular. "This is not a safe place for you," Thor said. "Too many plans. Too many schemes. Go to the Tower. I will meet you there in three days."

"Loki promised that you'd help me."

"And I will. Of that, you have my word. For now, however, no one can know where Loki is and where he is going. We must act in secret, remain in the shadows. In three days I will come for you."

"She needs rest." Bembuldir pointed at Shiara. "We haven't eaten in three days."

"The Tower is stocked with everything you need." Thor looked toward the fruit bowl placed on his table. "It's not a long journey," he said as he passed Bembuldir two green apples. "It's the best I can do for now. Whatever you need to rebuild the farm, you'll get it. I need you to wait. Once this entire ordeal is over, you have my word, you'll get everything you need."

CHAPTER THIRTEEN

"MY LIEGE," said Angrboda, "I meant no disrespect. Long have we awaited your foretold return to us. It is my honor to be in your presence."

Loki stood perplexed. The woman, who only moments ago had been pointing an arrow at his head, now knelt in front of him, her voice not louder than a whisper. *Well, that worked better than I thought,* Loki reflected as he scratched his beard, covering a smile with his hand.

"Please get up," he said as he allowed himself to sink back onto the bed.

Angrboda stood, her head still pointed toward the floor. "It is just as the shaman Grimnir prophesied. You have come back to us. May you now rid us of the faithless pretenders that scourge our lands."

Loki couldn't hold back the laugh. "The shaman Grimnir?! Well, I take it Odin's mission to travel the realm and live among the people extended far beyond the reaches of Asgard." Though Angrboda's head remained lowered, Loki could see the palpable look of confusion on her face. "There is no Grimnir," he said. "Hope is a form of control. Years ago, after the war, Borr, king of Asgard, sent Odin on a mission. The public pretext for this mission was that Odin was to 'travel the realm, live among the people, for a king that does not know his people is no king at all.' During the mission, he took the name Grimnir as an alias. I always had my suspicions that Odin's mission had more to it than what we were told. They said he was a master of disguise, but this—to trick an entire nation that their long-stolen king would one day return—is an impressive feat." The woman looked up at him. "There is no prophecy, Angrboda. There never was." He furrowed his brow and scratched his temple. "Wait, what was that last part about faithless pretenders?"

Angrboda remained silent for a moment and lowered her head once more, not as a sign of reverence this time, but rather to collect herself and her thoughts. "Many have claimed to be the lost son of Farbauti. Others believed that the Aesir would've killed the would-be king by now and so proclaimed themselves. None have found success. Those who remember, remember well the times of the king. Although I can't remember it—I was but a child during the war—I can remember an easier world, one with less hate, less killing. The war broke us, Loki. No food. No one who'll trade with us. And what did we do to deserve it? I may not remember the war all too well, but its aftermath is the reality of our everyday. The prophecy that one day you would return, and everything would be as it once was, it was the only thing that gave us hope in the darkness. And now you mean to tell me it was all a lie? If Grimnir's prophecy is not true, then why are you here?"

"I'm here to stop another war," Loki said. "There has been an attempt on Thor's life, the heir to Asgard's throne. It was a Jotunn. Somehow he'd managed to venture into Asgard undetected. While I believe it to be the work of one man, Odin believes the attempt was part of some larger plot against the Aesir crown. He's preparing his army for war as we speak." He paused for a moment. "If you are looking for a king, look elsewhere. Odin gave an oath to his dying father that he would never harm me. That means if he doesn't know where I am in Jotunheim, he won't attack out of fear of breaking his oath. If I am to do what you want me to do, Odin would know exactly where I am. The man has eyes and ears everywhere. Unfortunately, he doesn't trust most of them. But if I am to return to Utgard and take my father's throne, he'll burn everything else, leaving only that one solitary fortress standing."

"But you could unite us," Angrboda said. "Without the Vanir by his side, we could defend ourselves; we could take him."

"I don't want it," Loki said. "Kingship is nothing more than a fable we tell ourselves, that so and so is special and fit to rule because he is the son of so and so. You want me to lead you, but you have no idea who I am or if I'm even fit to rule."

She looked at him and said, "How did you escape?"

"I walked out the front door."

"Excuse me?"

"Walked. Out. The. Front. Door." Loki placed his palm on Angrboda's shoulder. "Being a prisoner doesn't mean you're in chains. Odin used to believe that one day, he'd send me back to Jotunheim to take the throne. Jotunheim would then be an independent kingdom in name only, with a puppet in charge and Asgard pulling all the strings. Then, plans, as they tend to do, changed. I became counsel to Thor. Say what you will about Odin, but Thor is a good man. When he is king, he will see it done, by heeding the words of his counsel, that trade with Jotunheim be opened once more. The starvation will end."

"He has told you this?"

"No, but I'm his counsel, and as long as it doesn't involve hitting someone over the head, he tends to listen to what I tell him."

Angrboda walked backward, grabbed the arrow from the floor, and sat cross-legged on one of the wooden chairs beside the fire. "If what you are telling me is true, why are you here?"

"I'm here to find evidence, and by evidence, I mean a Jotunn mad enough to testify before Odin that no one has laid claim to the throne of Jotunheim and that there is no Jotunn plot to invade Asgard. To avert war, I see no other option."

"You speak like them," said Angrboda. "I remember how the soldiers spoke when they came to our village during the war. Took what they wanted, food and women. When they said it, that word,

'Jotunn,' they say it as you do, as if we were something else, as if we weren't human. You say it just like they did."

Loki stared at the fire, saying nothing. He let out a grunt as he lifted himself to stand, a hand placed on his back the entire time. "I am a foreigner wherever I go," he mused, outstretching his arms to warm himself in front of the flames. "Will you help me?"

CHAPTER FOURTEEN

THE CATACOMBS beneath the castle were an ill-kept secret. Loki, who had a penchant for appearing in one place then shortly another during his youth, had made it his prerogative to memorize them. The long, seemingly endless, dark, and damp corridors were as an artery through the body of the castle. They crept up from underneath the ground and blossomed into the walls of every quarter, providing a route of escape when the time would call upon it. Thor was not as familiar with the catacombs as Loki, though familiar enough; he had also taken to using them during his youth, albeit for very different purposes than Loki, sneaking chambermaids who tickled his fancy up to his room (this was long before he'd married Sif).

"Turn right three times, left, right again, walk fifty paces, climb, then walk straight," Bembuldir told himself, looking down at Shiara's silhouette, a small frame masked in darkness. The catacombs had been built many generations ago, during the height of the Aesir–Vanir war. If the castle were to be attacked, the catacombs, which provided an exit to the nearby forest, would offer an acceptable evacuation route. Never in their existence had they been used for such an end. They would, however, provide a suitable path for Bembuldir and his daughter to make their way out of the castle undetected.

He repeated Thor's instructions in his head as he marched onwards, taking the first of the three right turns. Shiara gripped her father's arm tightly, finding her legs sometimes dragging, unable to keep up with Bembuldir's pace. The air was thick with the scent of moisture and rot. As their eyes failed them, the farmer and the girl passed their hands upon the wet stone wall. If they could not see a turn, they hoped they would at least be able to feel it. As Bembuldir marched forward, making another two right turns and turning left, the weight on his arm grew heavier. He contemplated stopping to let the girl rest, but kept on moving. He turned right and began to count his steps, one, two, three, four, all the way to fifty. Then came the stairs, steep, slippery, and wet, climbing up them on all fours. A light breeze replaced the cold stillness of the catacombs as they reached the top. It was easier to breathe now. The girl sat on the floor, her gasps audible. Bembuldir summoned what strength he had left, grunted as he lifted her, and walked. In the dark, time was figureless, a dancing mistress begging to be found but staying hidden. After what seemed like half a day, with aching limbs and a sore back, he thrust the door open. Bembuldir squinted at the piercing light of day, shaded only by the towering trees.

It was only then, when they'd reached the forest, that Bembuldir allowed himself to rest. He leaned his back against the trunk of a tree and stretched his legs forward. Shiara wordlessly pulled at the bag on her father's shoulders. The farmer pulled out the two apples that Thor had given them. He bit, and there was an audible crunch. He chewed the mouthful slowly, spreading the flesh upon his tongue to make sure. A tear made its way down his cheek as he came to the realization that, yes, these were indeed *his* apples. Shiara looked at him and smiled, taking a bigger bite than most other girls her age even could. They ate slowly. Here, tired and alone in a foreign land, in this one unspoken moment, they were back on the farm.

Bembuldir leaned his head back and let the world drift into black. In his dream, he saw her. In his dream, he was home. Limtra would be cooking rabbit stew, or maybe it would be kidney pie today. He would be out on the fields tilling his crops, only coming home as the sun drifted too close to the horizon. He would then call her name as he entered; she would greet him with a smile and a kiss on the cheek. She didn't this time. Instead, she was busy at work. He called her name once again, and once again, she didn't reply. She just stared at him. Blood began to flow from her neck. Tears flowed freely from her eyes. The house started to shake. Then came the scream, terrible and piercing.

Bembuldir awoke to find his daughter climbing on top of him, her face pale and her eyes bloodshot. A searing, throbbing ache bore its way through the farmer's core. "It hurts," said the girl, gripping her stomach tight. "It hurts so much." She lost her balance and slipped, coughing into her little hands. Staring at the scarlet liquid in her palms, her lips began to quiver. "Daddy?" she whimpered, raising a bloody palm.

"No, no, no," gasped Bembuldir before keeling over. It was as if a sword had been thrust into his side. "No, no, please." These were not the words of a strong, determined man. These were the words of a man watching his daughter die, and finding himself helpless to stop it. "No, please, take me! Take me, not her. Please, please, not her." He bit his lip as hard as he could and rubbed his daughter's hair. "It's alright," he lied. "It'll be alright." It was then that he noticed that she'd stopped moving.

The howl came out of him like a raging fire burning through a dry forest, only for it to be silenced by the burning inside of him. "No, please," he said, holding the little body, which already felt colder than it had been only moments ago. "Not like this. Not like this. Not like this. Not like this. Not like this!" It threw him, involuntarily forcing him away from his little girl. He writhed where he lay, wishing for it all to end. And then it did.

CHAPTER FIFTEEN

THE CLAY HUT had no windows, making it impossible to decipher whether it was day or nighttime. The glow of the fire flickered on Angrboda's face as she sat cross-legged, staring at nothing in particular. She sighed, stood up, and walked toward the door. The cold filled the room as the door creaked open. She nodded her head toward Loki.

It was not a town. It may have been, once upon a time, but now it was nothing of the sort. Angrboda's hut was one of many, though most were missing their roofs. There were no voices. No sound but the hiss of the wind. The remains of what looked like it once was a shop lay not too far away from Angrboda's hut. "That used to be a butcher's. And that over there, that used to be a smithy. The miners quarters were there."

"What happened here?" said Loki, taking small, slow steps as his arm drifted from his back. He leaned down and grabbed at the half-burned, snow-covered soil.

"The war happened." Angrboda motioned with her head for Loki to follow. "A war never ends when people think it ends. When Asgard saw to it that no other nation would trade with Jotunheim, people banded together, hoping beyond hope that there'd be enough to go around. There wasn't. This land is barren. Rain comes scarcely. No matter how much we worked, we could not grow enough. As time passed, people grew angry, desperate. Then the killing started. Marauders made their way through the land, taking what little we had picked dry. Those that dared ventured into Midgard, with caution at first. With time, raids grew more frequent. Killing became a sport. You come here asking for my help to stop another war. For you, the war ended twenty-four years ago. For us, it never ended."

They walked beyond the rows of half-charred houses and shops, some with their signs still intact. Then came a small fence, followed by a seemingly unending field of broken and anonymous headstones. The cemetery gate creaked as Angrboda pushed it open. It was hard for Loki to guess at the number of graves in front of him. Some—those with larger headstones—were easy to see. White covered the smaller headstones, obscuring them from view. As he walked, he counted. Then, when he'd reached a hundred, he stopped counting.

The three graves were different than the others. The headstones weren't damaged. Atop them were freshly cut hellebore, hearty flowers that didn't mind the cold. Angrboda closed her eyes and began to whisper something inaudible under her breath.

"Who are they?" Loki asked.

"I wasn't always alone. This place used to be full of so much life. We didn't have much. We'd often sleep hungry. But we always had each other. When the raids started, they said they'd be over soon. That people would come to their senses. It never happened. When they came, they had no mercy. I remember laying in a pool of my own blood, unable to move as they killed them. There," she pointed at the largest of the graves, "lays Jormungandr. We'd married when I was twelve. I was the older one. He was eleven. Four years later, we had a son. We called him Fenrir after the Great Wolf that shelters those under the sky. Our second-born, we called him Loki, after the rightful king, the one who would finally bring peace to our lands."

"I am so sorry," said Loki. "Who buried them?"

"I did," Angrboda said. "It nearly killed me, carrying them one by one. I thought of giving up. But they deserved it. To find some semblance of honor and dignity in death, the sort they hadn't been afforded in life. I stayed up for nights on end, thinking about why it was that I survived. Why destiny had chosen me. Then I came to believe that there was no such thing as destiny. That life is cruel, nothing but suffering. That only once life has taken everything from you do you get a hole in the ground, an end as food for the maggots and the worms. But then. . . ." She paused for a moment. "But then I found you. The heir to Jotunheim. No matter what you say, whether that prophecy is nothing but a lie, that I survived and found you, there is some reason for it. I have to believe it. I have to."

Loki looked down at the snow covering his feet. "What is destiny but the space between the road we choose and the one we don't?" He placed his hand on Angrboda's shoulder. "I wish it were different, but the road behind us has been paved. The only question any of us have any right to ask is how we are to pave the road in front of us. I cannot be your king. But what I can do is try to make things better. If you come with me, we can prove to Odin that Jotunheim is innocent. We might even be able to convince him to open up the trade routes."

"You're asking me to grovel at the feet of the man that killed my family. He may not have slit my son's throat, or cut my husband in two, but it was he that built such desperation in people that they forgot that they were human."

Loki lowered his hand. "And what's the alternative? Odin is preparing for war, right now, as we speak. I can't undo what happened. I wish I could. But right now, we have a chance, a fighting chance, to save thousands of lives. No matter how bad things are now, I can guarantee you another war will only make it astronomically worse."

"If I am to do what you're asking me to do, I'll have forsaken everything they stood for. To be a nation that stands on its own two feet. What you're asking me to do, to bow my head to the throne of Asgard—" She kneeled forward and placed her hand on the largest of the three graves. "—it would mean dishonoring them."

"I wouldn't ask this if I saw any other way. To do something you don't want to do, something that churns your stomach, making you feel physically ill, but doing it for the greater good, doing it because you know that it's the best option you have open to you, doing it because it's right, that's what's called compromise."

She remained kneeling, her eyes closed as the blowing snow sprayed her jet black hair in white. "What guarantee do you have this will work?"

Loki shook his head. "None."

"So you want me to betray everything I stand for, and you can't guarantee success." Her body still facing her husband's grave, she turned her head toward Loki and, with a half-hearted nod, said, "Long live the king."

CHAPTER SIXTEEN

ALTHOUGH THEY WERE dark and damp and cold and sometimes foul-smelling, the catacombs had always been, for Thor, a happy place. As a boy, he and Loki would often play find-find, a game not too dissimilar from hide-and-go-seek. Loki and Thor would walk into the tunnels that stretched through the body of the castle at different points. Then, each would try to find the other without being seen himself. It was a game that Loki enjoyed far more than all others, chiefly because it was one of the few games he could beat Thor at. Thor, in turn, loved the game also, but not for the game itself; he enjoyed games of a physical nature a great deal more. Rather, he appreciated it because of the utter joy on Loki's face when he'd caught him—which he usually did.

But this time, as Thor walked in the dark of the catacombs, he could not find any joy in himself. The last few weeks had been, to put it mildly, irritating. Although he was now back to full health, Odin did not force Baldr to relinquish the title of Master of Arms. Publicly, Odin would say that it was because Thor hadn't fully recuperated and was in no shape to lead Asgard's armies. But Thor knew this wasn't the case. Upon finding out that Thor knew Loki's whereabouts and that Loki's whereabouts were Jotunheim, Odin had begun to question the integrity of his eldest son. It irked Thor that Baldr, whom he'd expected to make a royal cockup of things, was doing a far better job than anyone had expected. Nevertheless, Thor found comfort in two matters, the first being his unwavering belief in Loki. Any day now, he believed, Loki would arrive back at the castle with a trustworthy witness, and this whole blasted matter would be over and done with. The other being Frigg, Odin's second wife. Frigg had made Odin swear that no harm shall ever befall Baldr. Thus, Odin would never charge Baldr with actually commanding Asgard's armies in battle. To prepare them for war was one thing, but to lead them into combat was an altogether different matter.

Thor closed his eyes as he walked, pushing his palm into the wall, reaching for the upcoming right turn. He felt it, turned, walked fifty paces, got on all fours, and began to climb. As he made his way, he felt the cool of the outside air drape itself about his back. Then came the long walk forward, and after that, the door. A moment after he opened the door, he fell to his knees, looked around to make sure no one was watching, and wept.

They lay there, unmoving, motionless, blue, and cold in pools of red. With her eyes closed, the girl looked as though she might have been sleeping. The man, on the other hand, had a palpable look of dread frozen on his face. He was meant to protect them, not lead them to their deaths. Then, his eyes drifted to the two green, blood-soaked apples. His lips quivered as he came to the stark realization that this cruel fate had not been meant for them. It was meant for him.

But this was not the time for thoughts of plotting or conspiracy.

Thor hoisted the man onto his right shoulder and girl onto his left, turned, and marched back through the cold and damp. This was no longer a happy place. At that moment, the catacombs transformed into a thing altogether unholy: It was the place where Thor had led an innocent man and a little girl to their deaths.

Guilt is an awful thing. What makes it a truly odd feeling is that one can feel guilty of committing a crime one had no part in. Like two intertwining serpents, the guilt that pumped itself through Thor's veins found itself tangled with another emotion, one far simpler but often more devastating: rage.

The water garden was a sacred place. There, only princes, heroes, and martyrs were entombed. It was the mark of high virtue and nobility to be buried there, a place for those who spent their lives giving, sacrificing themselves but becoming more beautiful in doing so. There, in the water gardens, their bodies sustained the water lilies, which glimmered in the night with colors of blue, purple, and white. There, in the water gardens, they would continue their good works in death, as they had done in life.

As Thor waded in the water and dug, a crowd began to form. They hadn't seen the young prince in many months. However, their attention was on the body of the man dressed in white and the child lying beside him. Thor had washed Bembuldir and Shiara's bodies and dressed them in white, a sign of high regard in Asgard.

Though he held no great title, bore no great lineage, and had meager wealth, many of the guards, handmaidens, and helpers knew Bembuldir. He would ride up to the castle on his donkey (who had the unfortunate task of dragging three carts' worth of produce) with a large smile on his face. He would often joke with those who had the pleasure of dealing with him. Not a soul in Asgard bore any ill will to Bembuldir, yet there he lay, and alongside him, his daughter.

The crowd offered their help. Thor took none. This was his burden, his responsibility, his failure. There was no eulogy, only the hushed whisper of gossip and rumor.

Thor sat alone that night, eating and drinking nothing, half out of guilt, confusion and rage, and half out of fear. He didn't want to believe it. But then again, he hadn't seen Baldr since he'd left the medical bay. It could've been a perfect crime, and some part of Thor wished it had been.

At the crack of dawn, an ungodly hour reserved only for slaves and thinkers, Thor made his way to the field. The soldiers had yet to wake. Some slept in tents, others on the bare ground. Unending rows and rows of them. Among the army should've been a group—not a battalion but a troop of fifty—who were never allowed to be asleep at the same time. They were the crème de la crème of Asgard's military might. No one knew why they had come to be called the Fifth Troop, but what was known was that the Fifth Troop had one task and one task only: to serve under the Master of Arms and to obey his orders, no matter what he asked.

In times past, as the Aesir-Vanir war went on, the relationship between the Master of Arms and those serving in the Fifth Troop had become a brotherhood. They fought together, ate together, laughed together, and mourned together. Thor, having been appointed with the mantle during a time of peace, had no such comradery with the troops; instead, although they would never mention it to his face, the Fifth Troop found Thor to be brutish, lacking the strategic mind of previous masters, and—in their view his greatest weakness—far too dependent on his counsel. As they had no love for Thor, Thor had no love for them. To him, they were nothing more than a nuisance, bloodhounds searching for something—anything—to kill, with a philosophy and a demeanor ill-suited to peacetime.

Thor scoured the field, looking for one of the Fifth Troop, easily identifiable by their clunky and far too well-polished armor, but they were nowhere to be found. Nearby, lying in the grass, was a man sleeping. His shield lay beside him, its green-and-blue-emerald-covered shoulder pads a dead giveaway that the man was a lieutenant. Thor grabbed him by the scruff of his shirt, pulling him in an instant from sleep's gentle embrace. Then, in a manner more polite than one would expect, Thor asked the lieutenant for Baldr's and the Fifth Troop's whereabouts. The man said that he didn't know. Thor asked him who did know, far less politely this time. The man pointed to his superior, a general who was fast asleep in his tent a few paces away. The general, though groggy and half hungover, gave Thor all he needed to know in just two words.

"Where's Baldr?"

"Gone."

"And where is he going?"

"Jotunheim."

CHAPTER SEVENTEEN

ODIN'S FOOTSTEPS echoed through the counsel chamber. He held his hands behind his back as he paced, a look of deep contemplation masking the fear and the anger inside. "How long?" he asked.

"Six days," said Thor. "Baldr has not been seen in six days."

Mimir placed his palm to his temple; his elbow pressed firmly on the table. "Sire, though it is unsanctioned, Loki's mission is our best hope for a peaceful resolution to this debacle. Baldr's interference will put the entire mission in jeopardy." He turned to Frigg, Odin's wife and Baldr's mother, who was sitting beside Mimir. He outstretched his palm to her, and she gripped it tightly. "Not to mention, the prince's safety."

"Foolish boy," mumbled Odin to himself as he continued to pace back and forth.

Frigg's grip tightened around Baldr's hand. She turned toward Odin. "You swore to me that no harm shall ever befall my son. Now look what's happened."

"I would see that oath broken," said Thor. "Your son tried to kill me. He murdered an innocent man and a little girl in the attempt."

"You have no evidence of that," Frig said.

"I'm afraid that we do," Mimir said, feeling Frigg's grip upon his hand loosen then recoil. "A handmaiden, under Baldr's orders, delivered the apples to Thor's quarters. Two apples. I might not have seen the deceased, but the description given to me of their bodies indicates that they were poisoned with Siperian Vialum, a concoction at least four members of the Fifth Troop have the knowledge to make. His disappearance only acts as a further indictment."

"Do you hear this, Odin?" Frig gasped. "Are you hearing what they are saying about our son?"

"I am," Odin whispered.

"And do you believe them?"

"I do." His pacing ceased, and he turned toward his wife. "I should have seen it. To be given no power at all, then all of it at once . . . what it must do to a man." He paused momentarily. "This is my fault," he said. "To keep a man from all harm, that is a harm in itself."

"Please," Frig begged, "he is the only son the gods have blessed me with." That was, of course, not true. She had been blessed with two sons, Baldr and Hod, but, to her dismay, Hod was born blind. He might've grown up to be kind and honorable. No one will ever know. One night, when the child was still not a year old, Frig, believing that she was doing her younger son a kindness, protecting him from the world, placed a pillow atop the boy's head and pressed down.

Odin turned to Mimir. "Counsel, old friend, what do you think I should do?"

Mimir squinted, rubbing his eyebrows with his thumb and index finger. "There is only one thing that can be done. Baldr must be stopped. If he enters Jotunheim and is killed, it will mean war. If he finds Loki, he'll jeopardize your brother's mission, meaning that we will be no closer to ending this dreadful matter. Baldr must be stopped. There is no other way. Whether you wish to hold him accountable for his actions is another matter entirely, one that we can discuss at a later date. We must do what is right for the realm. You must do what is right for the realm. And what is right for the realm is to avoid war unless it is absolutely necessary. Loki's actions, no matter what you think of them, were for the good of the realm. You know this."

"Father," Thor said, his voice barely a whisper, "let me go after him. Alone." He turned to Frig. "I won't harm him. By the gods, I want to, but I won't. You have my word."

Frig spat on the floor. "I wouldn't trust one with Jotunn blood to bring my son home safely. You should be grateful that your king did not declare Baldr as the true heir to Asgard. After all, he's Odin's only pure-blooded son."

"Enough!" Odin slammed his fist on the table. "Speak to him in such a manner again, and I will have your tongue cut out." His face was red. "Thor, by the command of your king, you are reinstated with the title of Master of Arms, and as such are burdened with the task of returning Baldr to the castle unharmed. Go alone or not—you have command of Asgard's army. Take all you need, but return my son to me unharmed."

CHAPTER EIGHTEEN

CLOUDS ROLLED over the moonless dark sky as an eerie orange glow illuminated the horizon. Baldr could feel an immeasurable pressure within him pushing upon his very being, an unknown lifeless force draining every inch of joy. It was as if the earth itself had engulfed him, drowning him beneath the tar-soaked soil. All around him were trees of a sort he did not recognize. Though he knew better than to do so, having done it countless times before, he could not resist the urge to snap his fingers. As it sometimes did, the spark started the fire. He felt himself pushed further into the ground as the fire burned the forest around him. He tried to yell, to scream for help, but his voice was gone. It always left him in this unholy place, every time.

He opened his eyes to see a forest quite different from the one in his dreams. Having moved far too much in his sleep, his cheek was planted on the damp soil, his sleeping bag several steps away. He looked up at the man standing guard. The man lowered his head and looked away. To his left and his right, Baldr's men, the Fifth Troop, lay sleeping. It was the middle of the night, and Baldr knew sleep had banished him from her abode. He stood up and walked toward the man watching over the others, informing him he would stand guard instead. The man smiled and refused, saying he would be honored if they stood guard together.

The men of the Troop found in Baldr the leader they wished Thor had been. They believed he was smart and cunning, but most of all, they found his cold demeanor to be a reliable indicator that he took his responsibilities seriously (the same, they thought, could not have been said of Thor). At long last, the men of the Troop had found something they had been seeking for over two decades: purpose. During peacetime, those that crave war find themselves going through a process not too far removed from that of an addict missing his vice of choice.

The men rose with the sun. First, they would take their morning meal. During that time, the scout would go out looking for tracks. Several days ago, the scout had brought news that troubled Baldr. The tracks didn't belong to one man. They belonged to two. Baldr searched his mind, wondering who might be accompanying Loki. Though he thought and he searched, he could not think of anyone. In his head, he began to question the scout's assessment. Perhaps the tracks belonged to someone else? In any case, he said nothing, knowing tracks were the only thing Loki would be dumb enough to leave behind.

Following their morning preparations, the Fifth Troop would then march until darkness took the day and there was very little to see. As they walked, they would sing songs, war songs, songs that hadn't been sung in over twenty years. As the soldiers around him sang that day, Baldr's thoughts turned toward his brother, and then his future.

A sinking ache grew in his stomach; not pain, but something of a similar nature. It was not entirely unpleasant, but neither was it plea-surable. He yearned to see it—the source of all his troubles, on the floor, lifeless, in a pool of blood. Thor had been, Baldr thought, his one real impediment to greatness. Had it not been for Thor, he would've been the heir to Asgard's throne. Had it not been for Thor, his mother wouldn't have made Odin swear that no harm would befall him. Had it not been for Thor, he would have never been a shadow, a figure in the darkness grabbing at the light. Some small part of him regretted it had to be this way; then again, it was only a tiny part. One he had long considered merely background noise.

Following Thor's tragic demise, thought Baldr, Odin would have no choice but to name him as the permanent Master of Arms and heir to Asgard's throne. He would see to it that Jotunheim was brought to heel. Tales of his conquest would echo through the ages. Songs would be sung of Baldr the Brave. Toasts would be made to his name for centuries to come. Just as the Fifth Troop had seen his wisdom, the world would recognize it too. A leader, strong and fierce, but fair.

Nothing less than the greatest king the world had ever seen.

CHAPTER NINETEEN

As THEY WALKED, day after day, the cold began to lessen. Beneath them, white, snow-covered earth turned, with each passing footstep, to black soil. It was a paradoxical land, a place that hung between the two realms, not quite Midgard and not quite Jotunheim. The earth was rich, but cold stopped anything from growing. Except for the tree. A singular figure, the lone source of brown and green in an otherwise colorless tundra.

Angrboda passed her fingers through the long, thin, prickly leaves. Loki, on the other hand, walked past it without even a passing glance. Only after he was several feet ahead did he notice that the sound of footsteps behind him had stopped.

"Come on," Loki said as he turned to look back. "It'll be dark soon."

"I came here when I was a girl." Angrboda picked a small yellow flower from the tree and put it to her nose. "This is the farthest I've ever been from home. I always wanted to see the world. And now I'm about to. I wish it could have happened differently."

He was about to tell her to get a move on and that he had no interest in finding out what creature that howling noise in the distance belonged to. The expression on her face changed his mind. "I always wanted to visit Jotunheim when I was a boy," he said. He walked toward her. "When I got a little older, I thought I never would. Now that I'm here, I wish that it was under different circumstances. Plus, being speared in the back and having my horse turned into stew was hardly the royal welcome I was expecting."

"It was good stew, though," Angrboda said with a smile as she picked the petals from the flower.

"That's my friend you're talking about." He put on a look of false outrage. "We'd be in Asgard right now if he was still alive."

"Well," Angrboda said, letting the petals fall to the ground, "I guess it's a good thing we ate him. I want to enjoy the view." Her smile then faded. "I just wish they could have been here with me."

"Your family?"

"Aye, without family, the world loses half its beauty." She pulled her shoulders up, walking past Loki, away from the tree. "Come on then. We'd best get out of here before nightfall. Unless you want to be dealing with a dire wolf."

By nightfall, they reached the forest. Angrboda slept, bathed in the moonlight. For a moment, Loki caught himself not looking at her, but seeing her. Well and truly seeing her. The small scar next to her left eye. Her long jet black hair, in stark contrast to her milky skin. He looked at the ground and cursed himself. She let out a small groan and opened her eyes.

"What is it?" she said as she pulled herself upright.

"Can't sleep," he said. "Too much going on up there." He pointed to his head.

"What's got you worried?" she asked.

"Nari, my son. When I left, I did everything I could to push every thought of him and his mother aside. Odin swore he would never harm me. He never said anything about them. If he sees this, me running away, me coming here, as some sort of betrayal. . . ." Loki clenched his palm into a fist and pressed it to his lips. "After all these years, Odin doesn't trust me. Not fully. He never wanted me to be Thor's counsel. But when Thor sets his mind on something, there's not much that can be done to change it. If Odin thinks I've betrayed him, what if he does something to them? To my family? They're my family. I'm supposed to protect them. How can I protect them if I'm not there?"

She placed her hand on his. "I know what it's like to fear for family and be completely and utterly powerless to protect them." She felt Loki's fingers intertwine with hers. "Your voice changes when you mention his name. Thor, I mean."

"He's the only friend I have. He's the only one I know that I can trust to protect them. My teacher, Mimir, he's like a father to me. But he can't protect them. Thor can."

"Sleep," Angrboda said. "Or at least try to. You'll need your strength." She then turned away, placed her head on the cold soil, closed her eyes, and drifted off.

He stared up at the trees and the full moon, his mind a raging whirlwind of desperation, guilt, and purpose. Sleep would not find Loki until only an hour before dawn.

CHAPTER TWENTY

BALDR CIRCLED his fingers around the stein's rim. In the corner of his eye, he saw a man whom he hadn't seen in many years. All around the man were empty mead tankards. A rotund woman sat on his lap. Baldr smiled and even contemplated leaving the man be. After all, he'd never seen Heimdall so happy.

The tracks led him here, to the town of Fildred, and then they ended. Each man of the Troop was handed a hefty sum and told to do with it as they pleased. The result was a display of debauchery on a scale large enough to put any modern-day university fraternity house to shame.

The Fifth Troop would take three days of rest in the town, ample time for the scout to find Loki's trail. They'd arrived two days ago, and the scout was no closer to his target. Baldr turned to the man sitting to his left and whispered something inaudible into his ear. The man turned to his comrades, seated a few tables away, and waved his fingers in the direction of the entrance. The two men nodded and walked toward the door.

Heimdall, who was too busy rubbing his face between the fat woman's breasts, hadn't noticed the squeal of the chair moving. The woman tried to scream, but the rope had already encircled her gullet.

A force pulled Heimdall to the floor, and he found his breathing restricted by Baldr's boot.

"Resist, fight back, refuse to tell me anything I want to know, the whore dies, understand?" said Baldr, pushing down just enough with his foot to allow Heimdall to nod. "Good." He turned to his men. "Get everyone out of here."

After some commotion, within moments the tavern was empty. The only injury dealt in the process was a broken nose to the barman. The rope, which had been tightly pressed along the woman's throat, made its way to Heimdall's wrists. Heimdall tightened and clenched his hands into fists as he was tied to the chair.

Baldr circled Heimdall as a buzzard circles a carcass. "I must say, I feel that the realm is truly in danger, now that the Watcher has abandoned his post." The woman lay on the floor, too frightened to move a muscle. "The Watcher is too valuable an asset to the realm, one that we cannot do without. As such, no harm should come to him." Baldr pulled his knife from the sheath. "I'm going to ask you some questions. Play any games, do or say anything I haven't asked you, and I'll cut off a piece of her." He leaned down and pressed the knife against the woman's sizable arm. "Who knows, might do this one a little good to lose some weight. Nod if you understand."

Heimdall nodded.

"Is he here?" Baldr pressed the knife just enough to hurt. "Nod if yes. Shake your head if no."

Heimdall shook his head.

"Do you know where he is?"

Heimdall shook his head once more then said, "But I know where he's going to be."

Baldr pressed the knife down. The woman's screams filled the room. "I thought I told you not to say anything unless I told you to." He pressed his knee to her back to stop the shaking and continued to cut.

"I'll tell you everything you want to know. Just let her go," Heimdall said. "She's got nothing to do with this. Please."

Baldr plunged the knife deeper this time. "What did I just tell you!"

He wrapped his hand around the woman's mouth to muffle the screaming. "Say or do anything I haven't told you, in the exact way I've told you, and I'll cut even more. Nod if you understand."

The screaming faded. Heimdall nodded, sunk into place, and unclenched his fists. He looked to the man on his right and the two standing by the door.

"Look at me," Baldr said as he wiped the blade on the woman's dress. "Where is he going? Say it."

"You haven't done this before," Heimdall said, motioning with his head toward the woman's lifeless body. "And you just lost your only leverage." The rope burned as he pushed himself out of his bonds. The man to his right swung. Heimdall ducked and grabbed the chair's feet, thrusting it forcefully into the man's chest. The two men by the door sprang into action, but it was too late. By the time they made their move, Heimdall had leaped out of the small window at the opposite end of the tavern.

The Troop searched every inn, food house, tavern, and brothel. Heimdall's whereabouts remained unknown for the rest of the day. As the Troop searched, they found nothing but their number reduced from fifty to forty-two. Two bodies were found at a local food store, four at different taverns in the area, and the rest at the Belvar Brothel, an establishment known to cater to more adventurous tastes.

That night, as he hid in a stable house, Heimdall contemplated leaving. Perhaps he might run away, finding peace in a far-off realm. Alas, a man's conscience often pulls him to do things he might one day regret. He would stay, he decided, and cut down as many men as he could. He rested his head on a bale of hay and slept.

The next day, the Fifth Troop was nowhere to be seen. Heimdall breathed a sigh of relief. He'd scared them off, or at least that was what he believed. In fact, Baldr had learned everything he needed to know when he met a somewhat disgruntled man during the search for Heimdall. "Greatest horse in the nine realms, and that bugger stole it from me." The man said that he couldn't remember the thief's name. Baldr asked the man to describe what the "bugger" looked like. "A

Jotunn. Small one. Smallest I've ever seen." It wasn't hard after that for the scout to find the horse's tracks.

CHAPTER TWENTY-ONE

IT WAS STILL early in the night. Angrboda sat by the fire, sharpening her blade while Loki slept. There was a rustle in a nearby bush. She readied her blade and quietly kicked Loki awake. Before he could speak, she pointed to the bush. They approached it with caution, swords at the ready. A squirrel leaped out from the bush and ran up a tree. Angrboda let out a sigh of relief and turned around to see a large man with red hair. She swung her weapon only to find her wrist caught midair. The man kicked her feet up from underneath her. On the ground, she looked up to see him admiring her blade.

"Who's this?" Thor asked with a smile on his face.

"A friend," Loki said before leaping at Thor, hugging him. "Good to see you."

Thor gently pushed Loki away. "As much as I would've liked this to be a warmer reunion, there's no time for talk." His smile faded. "Baldr's coming. He's got the Fifth Troop behind him, and he's out for blood. He's coming to kill you."

"Well, then bloody order them to stop," Loki said. "You're the Master of Arms. If you tell them to stop, they bloody well will have to."

"Baldr's spread his scouts all over the forest. It's impossible to avoid them." Thor raised his hammer. It was dripping with blood. "It seems that the Fifth Troop has no interest in following my orders. Had to take two out before I got here." He turned toward the woman. "Can she fight?"

"Aye," Angrboda said, "I can fight." She turned to Loki. "Who's this?"

"Thor," Loki said.

"The one you've been telling me about?"

Loki nodded.

"Good things, I hope," Thor said. "And you are?"

"Angrboda."

"Lovely name." Thor turned back to Loki. "We're going to need a plan of attack. Come on, counsel; this is your mission. What do you think we should do?"

"Why are you looking at me?" Loki said. "You're the one that's meant to be the great fighter. You tell me what we're supposed to do."

Thor chuckled. "Aren't you the one who told me that a man should plan for every eventuality, no matter how unlikely? And now you mean to tell me you have no idea how we're going to get out of this? Maybe I shouldn't have made you my counsel."

"Alright, alright," sighed Loki. "What's your plan?"

Thor grabbed a small branch from the ground and threw it into the fire. "We need to make it bigger."

"They'll see it," Loki said.

"That's what I'm betting on." Thor walked toward the flame. "Baldr's made sure to spread his troops just right, so that they're not too thinly spread, but that no one can get past them undetected. A fight is unavoidable. But, we can make the fight on our terms. Strip them of the element of surprise." He turned to Angrboda. "I promised my father I would return Loki and Baldr and, now I assume, by proxy, you, back to him unharmed. Take out as many of the Troop as you can, but Baldr, he's not to be harmed." He began to pace, then stopped midstride. "Well then, what are you two waiting for? Go get more firewood."

CHAPTER TWENTY-TWO

SLEEP WOULDN'T FIND him that night. How could it? This was it. This was the place. He'd seen it. A thousand times before and a thousand times again. Although he had never been here before, he knew it. He knew it like an old friend. Destiny, at long last, was at hand.

Smoke billowed above the treetops, dancing up and sideways. The men marched slowly, archers behind, swordsmen to the front. Moonlight lit the path, a glimmering shade of mystery, anxiety, and destiny.

The glow grew fierce, yet it was still far. Beyond the sound of crickets and dried leaves cracking under killer's boots, it called to him. A faint pull took Baldr. All around him, they continued to march.

A lone hooded figure stood by the fire. The flame was far too large to allow them to encircle him. Thor breathed deeply, readying the hammer. He took a step back, ensuring the shield was in place, then looked both sides. They had seen him, known who he was, yet they continued to march forward. He closed his eyes and began to count, hoping that the crackling embers would hide the trembling in his voice.

He took a deep breath to steady himself. "I am Thor, son of Odin, heir to the throne of Asgard and Master of Arms. By Odin's command, lower your arms and surrender my brother back to me.

Fail to do so, and I will show you no quarter." The marching ceased for but a moment before continuing precisely as it was. "Very well, then."

He raised his hammer. As it fell, it broke the closest man's shield and armor. Bleeding, the man stepped back and charged, screaming. The blunt force of the hammer cracked his skull in two. He dropped to the ground.

In the distance, the archers readied their bows. Thor motioned his foot toward the shield. "Nock," said a voice in the dark. The archers did as the voice commanded.

"Baldr, come out. End this madness," Thor yelled.

"Draw," called the voice. Thor could hear the sound of tightening rope.

"Baldr, it doesn't have to be this way."

"Loose!"

Thor kicked the shield's rim. It flew up, and he grabbed it. Arrows pierced the wood and steel. The force nearly knocked him backward. He dropped the shield as soon as the shooting ceased. Thor swung his hammer strong and true. He never thought he'd see the day he'd have to fight his own countrymen. "Nock," called the voice in the distance once again. Thor, who held his position, cried out his brother's name in rage as he prepared to strike the shield's rim once more. Thor lowered his head, allowing the spray of splinters to miss him. Following the second barrage, the shield could offer only a fraction of the needed protection.

"Woman," Thor said, surrounded on all sides. His hammer began to falter as his breathing quickened. "Now, blasted woman, now!" Angrboda emerged from the darkness, her blade in one hand and a sizable log in the other. The men of the troop broke ranks, unable to tame the attacks from the front and back.

In the distance, the voice cried "Nock!" once more. With all her might, Angrboda threw the log in front of herself and Thor. The arrows came, now in higher number, as the word "Loose!" filled the air. Shards of wood scattered in every direction. Then, a barrage of arrows flew in the other direction.

Out of sight, Loki marked the archers' locations. He gripped five arrows and fired them in quick succession. Thor broke position, pushing forward through the swarm of swordsmen. The thin steel of their swords and armor broke under the pressure of Thor's hammer. When they stabbed at him, Angrboda cut them down before their blades could find their target.

The archers fired their arrows every which way, trying to find who was shooting at them. No matter where they shot, the arrows kept on coming. Thor and Angrboda stood back to back as the swordsmen surrounded them. Without the help of the archers, their strength was significantly reduced. Then, the shooting stopped.

Finding no reprieve from Loki's aim, the archers fell back and circled the fight to the other side of the fire. Loki leaped into the battle, holding his arrows and his sword in one hand and bow in the other. For the experienced archer, the bow and arrow is not merely a long-range weapon, but also a weapon of devastating impact in close quarters. The troops found themselves fighting on two fronts. Near the flames, bodies began to pile up. Those that attempted to rush Loki were shot before they could get close enough to hit him.

The archers dipped the tips of their arrows into the flames on the other side and fired in any direction. Landing far too far away, the arrows posed no threat to the trio. However, hitting them directly was not the archers' intent.

The dry leaves, which coated the forest floor, provided a perfect fuel for the raging fire. Within mere moments, it grew in size and strength, covering everything that could be seen in an incandescent glow. The smell of roasted flesh clung to the air. Smoke bellowed from every direction. Loki's eyes burned, his aim growing worse as a result.

The men of the Troop began to run. As they did, they ran toward Loki; many didn't even give him a second glance as they made their escape. Thor and Angrboda remained back to back, each of them looking for the ideal moment to run.

Loki searched his mind for the best path to safety. "The Little Sea," he yelled through the chaos. "We have to get to the sea!" The Iving lay not a mile away from their location. Although the banks of the lake predominantly crossed Asgard and Jotunheim, the far western region was located in Midgard.

Thor nodded and ran forward to Loki. Angrboda followed suit. As they ran, the three of them, through the forest, Loki's memory of Heimdall's map their only guide, arrows followed them. "Show yourself," called Thor. "Show yourself, Baldr, and face me."

They tried to make for the downward pass but found it swarming with Baldr's men. With no other choice left, they made for the cliff's edge. Twelve men circled them. They could hear the waves crashing upon the rocks below. Thor raised his hammer, Angrboda her sword, and Loki his bow.

Their eyes filled with some unfathomable rage, the twelve rushed the three. Thor, panting, stood in front; Loki stood at the back, taking out four of the men before they could even get within striking distance. Smoke filling his eyes, Thor swung frantically. "Baldr, you coward, get out here and fight me!" Before Angrboda could even move, eight men lay dead at Thor's feet.

Unable to catch his breath, Thor fell to his knees. Loki closed his eyes and leaned forward, thinking of their best plan for escape. Then, all around them came the sound of marching. The men surrounded them. Thor stood and readied himself for the attack. It never happened. The men stood and waited.

Baldr too had waited—waited for years; waited for the opportune moment. And it was here.

Destiny was at hand.

CHAPTER TWENTY-THREE

OF THE ORIGINAL FIFTY, only fourteen remained. They drew their arrows and aimed at their targets. Thor took a step forward. A warning shot landed close to his feet. Loki stood perfectly still, his feet inches away from the cliff edge. He realized there was no way out, no plan of attack that didn't end up with all three of them dead.

A lone figure, cast in smoke and shadow, emerged. "The mighty Thor, bested," Baldr said as he walked past his men. "I thought you were dead."

"Sorry to disappoint," Thor replied, resisting the urge to leap forward and tear his brother limb from limb.

Baldr turned to his men. "If any of them move, shoot them." He proceeded to walk forward. "I've spent my entire life sheltered in your shadow. You were always our father's favored son. I was nothing more than a child in his eyes. Yet here we are. You believe yourself to be a great fighter, but you misunderstand the most fundamental law of combat. A man's soldiers must either love him or fear him. These men, they do not love you, nor do they fear you. They see in me what you could have never been: a leader. In all honesty, brother, I'm glad the poison did not kill you. For you to die knowing that it was weak, feeble

Baldr that bested you fills me with such warmth. At the end, all will know that Thor chose the Jotunns over his own people. They'll mourn for you, I'm sure. But in time, they will see your death as a blessing. After all, it is only because of your death that I may assume the mantle of heir."

It started as a light chuckle before transforming into manic laughter. Had he not been holding weapons, Thor would've gripped his sides due to the force of his mirth. "You can't win, brother. If you kill me, you lose. It was Odin that sent me here to find you, to bring you back. Though it hurts him to admit it, he is wise enough to see that Loki's mission is our best chance at peace. If you kill us, Father will not make you his heir. You will have left the line of Asgard broken. Father knows you tried to kill me. He also knows that a child and an innocent man died because you tried to poison me. The idea that you might return home and find yourself called a hero? Forget it. You can't win. I promised Father and your mother I would bring you back home unharmed. If you tell your men to stand down, I will hold to that promise. If you do not, I will cut all of your remaining men down, and you? I will kill you slowly. I will inflict such pain on you that you will beg me for death. And only then, as you lay bleeding, limbless, and blind, will I oblige your request and beat your skull in. So brother, tell me, what will it be? Face justice, or my wrath? The choice is yours."

A smile formed at the edge of Baldr's lips. He placed his palms behind his back. "Fourteen witnesses," he said. "Thirty-six dead, and fourteen witnesses to the Jotunn's crime." He turned back to face his men. "Honored brothers, loyal servants of the Aesir crown, did you see the Jotunn kill my brother?" The men nodded. "Did I not valiantly defend my brother?" The men nodded. "Knowing that the Jotunn had laid claim to the throne of Jotunheim, was I not left with no other choice but to kill him where he stood?" The men nodded.

Thor let out a blood-curdling roar and charged. He swatted the first arrow away with his hammer, but the second made its mark, piercing his chest. Then came another, and then another, and then another. Thor fell to the ground momentarily. Summoning every iota of strength left in his body, he got up before falling once more as Baldr's knife bore through his stomach.

"I wish I could say that I wish this had ended differently, but that would be a lie," Baldr said, standing over Thor. He outstretched his arm and gripped the broadsword handed to him by the soldier as tightly as he could. He could feel the damp forming at the heel of his boot. "Tears, brother, really? The mighty Thor dies crying. I thought I'd never see it."

"I loved you," Thor said.

Baldr looked up and stared Loki in the eye as he raised the sword. "Loki of Jotunheim, for the murder of Thor Odinson, I sentence you to die." With a speed he hadn't known was even possible, Loki fired. The arrow made its mark, striking Baldr's heart before the blade could fall. Baldr fell to his knees. In his final moment, he turned to face his men and saw it. The thing he'd seen a thousand times before. Something he'd dreaded. A lone unburnt shrub in a burning forest. He hadn't noticed it before. Had he seen it, he might've turned back. In a moment that passed as fast as the blink of an eye, but felt like an eternity, with his last wretched breath, he called to it. "Mistletoe."

It was as if the hands of time itself had stopped. The men, who could not have asked for a better opportunity to kill the three witnesses to their crimes, stood motionless in complete shock. Thor stared at the horrified expression frozen on Baldr's lifeless face. He gripped his hammer and stood. As if woken from a trance, the fourteen raised their weapons. Thor raised his, but before he could bring it down and take first blood, he felt the sharp edge of a knife pressed to his neck.

"Move an inch, and I'll kill him," Loki said, one hand gripping the knife's handle and the other the back of Thor's head. "Return home, and you'll be the men that saved Thor from a traitorous Jotunn. Move, and I kill him. I don't think Odin will look too kindly upon the men that let both of his sons die. Is that understood?" The men lowered their weapons.

With his arms still wrapped around Thor's neck, Loki began to walk backward slowly. Angrboda followed closely behind, Loki's bow in her hand, pointed squarely at the surviving men of the Troop. Thor's body grew heavy as he began to lose consciousness. When they were at last confident that they were out of sight, with what remaining strength he had left, Loki hoisted Thor onto his shoulder. The man's weight bore down on him, countered only by the adrenaline coursing through his veins.

Thor's breathing grew shallow as they reached the shore, blood flowing freely from the knife wound in his abdomen. With caution, Loki lowered Thor, applied pressure to the wound, and instructed Angrboda to tear a piece of cloth from his shirt. He wound it into a ball and pushed it down onto the cut. He took off his shirt and wrapped it around Thor's midriff, over the balled-up cloth. Then, he began to tend to the smaller wounds. It was midday before he was done. Angrboda stood watch the entire time on the off chance the remaining men of the Troop changed their minds.

"He's lost a lot of blood," Loki said as he finally stood, his knees throbbing, "but he'll live. He just needs rest. We'll wait here until he's fit enough."

"What if we don't?" Angrboda replied. "Come back with me to Jotunheim. Not as a king, but as a man. You're not one of them. Deny it all you want, but you know it to be true. You're one of us."

Loki leaned forward, remaining silent. He looked at her, then looked down upon Thor. Thor's eyes were closed, but his breathing had started to strengthen. Loki's lips quivered.

Many hours passed, and it was nearly nighttime. Thor opened his eyes and looked left, then right. No one was there. A light breeze formed and suddenly disappeared. There was no sound but the hush of waves caressing the land.

PART III
AN INTERLUDE THROUGH TIME

CHAPTER TWENTY-FOUR

THE WAVES EBBED AND FLOWED, freezing and melting as they crashed upon the shores of time. Thor stared out into the distance. The memory of this place shook him. He'd been here, on this very spot, five years prior, under very different circumstances.

He'd been bloodied, broken, and bruised. His brother had tried to kill him. He looked left and right, but no one was there. He called for Loki. The only reply he received was the echo of his own voice. He sat and waited, hours passing, each one longer than the next. *Perhaps they've gone to get help?* he thought. Night came. The wind howled and the wolves along with it. Thor searched for a weapon but found nothing. He lay his head on the cold earth, closed his eyes, and drifted into that vacuum between wakefulness and sleep.

He departed the next day, knowing that he'd been abandoned. Without a map, which he'd lost in the fighting, and with no recollection of this place, he meandered aimlessly, hoping that by some miracle his feet would point him in the right direction. As the days and nights grew colder and more bitter, and as the snow fell thicker, he knew they hadn't. There was nothing. A barren land fit for starvation. His eyes sunk into their sockets. The shaking grew feverish, incessant, and instinctual.

M.G. FARIJA

Then, the old man found him. Thor considered robbing him but saw in his possession nothing that might help his predicament. All the old man owned were the clothes on his back and a fishing line. "You look lost, son," the old man said to the skeletal frame that had once belonged to the fiercest warrior in the nine realms. "You're not from around here." Thor nodded. The old man decided that the disheveled person in front of him was, without doubt, an Aesir deserter, but didn't bother verifying the assumption. Instead, he invited Thor into his home—to heal, regain his bearing, and only depart when he was well and ready.

The old man, whose name Thor later found out was Samsur, didn't live in a town or a village, but alone in the wilderness, his wife and daughter his only company. "Safer this way," Samsur said. "You live somewhere people know, they come for you. Raiding and pillaging." He was right. Winters had started to grow colder and harsher, making it harder to grow what little could be grown. More and more people, though they hated themselves for it, reduced themselves to taking what was not theirs.

Life was hard but simple. In the vast, white wilderness, Thor found nothing of the luxury he'd been immersed in all his life. The house was made of broken stone, its uneven layers strengthening its structure. Due to the lack of surrounding forestry, a fire was a rare comfort. The cold, for all its bitterness, provided excellent food preservation conditions. That was all well and good as the winters, growing more vehement with every passing year, making the ice too thick to cut through, had virtually eliminated ice fishing in a few short years. Instead, Samsur made for the Iving to get his catch. It was relatively far, six days there and six days back. He carried salt with him, purchased in bulk years ago, to preserve the fish better. They didn't have much in the way of entertainment—just old songs which they mostly sang a capella. Sometimes, when the mood hit her, Jordubad, Samsur's wife, would break out the old kyling, a seven-string instrument not too dissimilar from a guitar. Their daughter, Jarnsaxa, had a majestic voice. Had she been born in modern times, she would have probably made her living singing soprano in the opera.

With long black hair that reached her waist, a long, deer-like neck, and thin red lips, she was no doubt beautiful. But it wasn't that which struck Thor. It was her voice. To him, it was as if a siren of Valhalla had descended to earth to serenade him.

Several months passed. Thor, who had more than recuperated, knew that it was time to leave. But deep inside, he felt a panging, a yearning for this life, one far away from schemes and politics. He asked Samsur if he could stay. "As long as you pull your weight," the old man said, "you can stay with us for as long as you want." And so Thor did. If he was asked to fish, he fished. If something needed mending, Thor fixed it. If singing was required, Thor sang (but was quickly told to be quiet).

After a year had passed, Thor, thinking that he'd never return to Asgard, finally plucked up the courage to ask for Jarnsaxa's hand in marriage. She was pregnant soon after the wedding. It was a boy. They called him Modi. About ten months after that, Jarnsaxa gave birth to a second son, Magni. Rarely did Thor's mind ever drift toward Sif, who could never bear him a child. Rarely did he even think of his previous life, if he did at all.

Three years passed before they saw the first of the Aesir soldiers. They marched around the Jotunn shores of the Iving. Thor kept himself hidden. They had been rumors that Aesir, clad in armor, had come to Jotunheim in search of someone or something. But Thor knew they were looking for him, or perhaps Loki. In all probability they were searching for both. By the fifth year, their numbers grew, and Thor knew that it was finally time to leave.

He stood on the banks of the Iving, staring out into the distance. The memory of this place shook him. He'd been here, on this very spot, five years prior, under very different circumstances. The waves ebbed and flowed, freezing and melting as they crashed upon the shore of time. Breaking, forming, colliding, until the mass turned into one. A frozen canopy. A bridge to back home.

CHAPTER TWENTY-FIVE

MIMIR STARED at the pile of letters on the table. *Send them out*, said a voice in the back of his mind. But to do so, he knew, was to sign his death sentence. He'd spent his life telling people to aim for a higher ideal, to fight for the greater good no matter the cost. No one listened to him much. Now, for the first time, as he stared death in the eye, he understood why. Of course, he knew that sacrificing your life for what is right was hard. But knowing it and facing it are two very different things.

He tapped them, making sure they were tangible, and counted them once again. *One. Two. Three. Four. Five. Six. Seven. Eight. All there.* It was treason, he knew, but if this meant the preservation of the realm, or at least its people, then he would not have qualms about being remembered as a treasonous wretch, if indeed anyone remembered him at all. History would burn too. It would all burn. After all, Ragnarok was coming. A violent rage, bursting forth from the land of Muspelheim, ready to devour Asgard whole.

It had taken a lot of research to come to this conclusion. Digging through Yggdra's history, its forgotten past, searching for answers in the dark. And when the answer finally came, a part of Mimir wished he'd never found out. It began fifteen years ago. Long before Loki's disappearance and Baldr's death had transformed the once mighty Odin into a wax statue of terror, a king clinging to his seat, hoping the wind won't blow him off.

Mimir began to recall his last conversation with Loki. His investigation, the one he'd half regretted embarking upon. It was still an intellectual curiosity then, an oddity that required further examination. He remembered telling Loki that they would look into the matter further when he returned. But Loki never returned. A ghoulish voice in the back of Mimir's mind told him that Loki was probably dead. He did his best to ignore it. The image of his own death was hard for him to conceive, but the image of Loki, alone and dead in a faraway land, that was an image altogether mortifying. He'd raised the boy, nurtured him from the age of barely one. More than anything, he hoped his ward, his son, was safe. He'd never find out, he knew. If news ever did come of Loki's whereabouts, he'd be long dead by then.

Fifteen years he was gone. But still, Mimir held out hope. Thor had been missing for five years before he returned, and he was fine, not a scratch on him. Maybe Loki was alright too; perhaps he'd found some idyllic life in Jotunheim and decided not to come back. But in his heart, Mimir knew Loki could never come back. He'd killed Odin's son. Yes, he did so to save Thor, but the fact remained: Loki had killed Baldr. Mimir closed his eyes, remembering the day Frigg found out that her son had been shot down like a wild animal. It tore her to pieces; it murdered her. Three years after that day, they'd found her in her bed, hanging, a rope around her neck. Odin couldn't forgive that.

One. Two. Three. Three kings. *Four. Five. Six. Seven. Eight.* Five elders. Eight letters. The first to King Hreidmar of Svartalfheim. The second to Freyr, king of Alfheim. And the third to Freya, queen of Vanaheim—a far better ruler than her father, King Njord, who did not wish to drag her people back into war. What responsibility Odin evaded, he hoped they might burden themselves with. The rest went to Asgard's town elders, who were only told to prepare themselves for the oncoming fire. (All but one, Bragi of Tilgrad, failed to heed his words.)

Mimir had spent years warning Odin of the calamity to come. Ragnarok was coming, sooner than one would think. The earth was breathing, readying itself to burst forth, smiting the land with molten rock and shattered shields. The king's counsel begged and pleaded. "Evacuate your people; our end is coming. Asgard is dead!" Odin called him a madman. For forty-eight years he'd been Odin's closest advisor, but it didn't matter. What Mimir spoke of, warned of, the mind could scarcely comprehend. To know, to believe, that everything you've worked toward, everything you've built is for naught, is not an easy linctus to swallow. It is far easier to call your friend a foe.

There was a knock on the door. Mimir lowered his eyes, his gazed fixed on the envelopes. He could throw them away, burn them, forget that he'd ever written them. It was now or never. "Come in," he said to the messenger. *All you have to do is hand them to him*, he thought. His hands shook, vibrating uncontrollably as he picked up the letters.

The words he'd told his ward hundreds, or possibly thousands, of times before came racing through his head. "You do what is right because it's right, not because it's easy." *Great advice to shell out. Much harder to follow*, Mimir thought. Difficult or easy, he followed it, placing the eight envelopes in the messenger's hands. "Only for the eyes of whom they are intended for, my boy. No one else." The messenger nodded. "If you're caught on the way, captured, imprisoned, no matter how unlikely, you burn them, throw them away, burn them. Only for the eyes of whom they are intended."

Every letter reached its destination safely. While the five chief elders of Asgard remained silent, the rulers of Svartalfheim, Alfheim, and Vanaheim came to their decisions. Independently, but unanimously, they'd agreed. The people of Asgard were welcome in their lands, and what assistance was needed for the evacuation would be supplied. When news of this finally came to Odin, he sent out another batch of letters, informing them that his counsel had grown old, senile, and incompetent.

Mimir was sitting on the balcony when they came for him. He offered no resistance but made one simple request. "Let me watch the sunrise one last time."

PART IV
FIMBULWINTER

CHAPTER TWENTY-SIX

TIME HAD NOT BEEN KIND to Jotunheim. In the forty-seven years since the war, trade with the other realms had been severely restricted. In turn, food, of which enough could not be grown locally, grew more and more scarce. Midgard faced the brunt of Jotunheim's desperation. Farmers banded together to defend themselves from Jotunn bandits and marauders, swearing to both Asgard and Vanaheim (which, for their part, did not care) that they would never sell or give their harvests freely. Such was the Jotunns' plight that many attempted to flee their homeland, only to find no other realm willing to accept them. In every town and village, the stench of desperation clung to the air—all except one.

The town of Hurrugane was located in the southernmost region of Jotunheim, some twenty miles away from Vanaheim and hundreds of miles away from Asgard. In comparison to the rest of Jotunheim, Hurrugane had a temperate climate. The rich, almost black, soil provided nutrients needed for farming. Moreover, the town lay half a mile away from the river Seltar, which extended from Vanaheim. The river provided the townspeople with a more than ample supply of salmon. In a word, Hurrugane was the only self-sufficient town in Jotunheim.

In the past, the town found itself the target of a great many bandits. But, for reasons none of the townspeople knew, not a single bandit had attacked them for over a decade. Surrounded by thick forests, the town should've been easy to spot.

Instead of asking too many questions, the townspeople were content to carry on fishing and farming, living in complete isolation of the turmoil swallowing the rest of their country.

Nothing much of interest happened in Hurrugane. If a family were to move in, which was rare, occurring only once or twice a year, they would be the talk of the town. The residents had very little interest in the people themselves; rather, they craved any news concerning the outside world. For all they knew, Jotunheim could now finally have a king (it didn't), or perhaps the Aesir or the Vanir had invaded once more (they hadn't), or maybe trade with the other realms had opened once again (it hadn't). As such, the townsfolk found themselves incredibly disappointed by the arrival of Thokk.

Thokk, the townspeople decided, was a peculiar and antisocial fellow. Rather than build his house within the village itself, he elected to build his home by the river. Thokk had a wife, Iárnvidia, and two sons, Fenrir and Jormungandr. He was a small fellow, the shortest Jotunn they'd ever seen. Not that they'd seen him much at all. Thokk only came to the village when necessity called for it. And every time he did, Byleistr, the town's blacksmith, found Thokk's interest in him and his two wards odd and even secretly troubling. Thokk was a quiet man, but whenever he frequented Byleistr's shop, it was as if he'd been replaced by someone else entirely. He would talk endlessly. Not only would he talk, but he would mention things about places Byleistr was quite positive no Jotunn had ever visited. Rather than voice his worries concerning Thokk, the smith kept quiet. After all, it might risk casting attention on Thokk's two wards, and if anything should happen to them, or if anyone were to learn who they were, the safety of Hurrugane itself would be at risk (along with Byleistr's hefty pockets).

In the five months Thokk had spent living near Hurrugane, he never invited anyone over. Moreover, whenever someone invited him over for dinner, Thokk would, in the most polite manner possible, refuse. Byleistr was both puzzled and surprised when, after many months, Thokk invited him over for dinner. A part of him wanted to say no, that he did not wish to be a burden. However, he also wished to know if Thokk was on to him. He accepted.

He tried to pace himself, but Thokk was insistent. Mead followed hot wine; every tankard was followed by another. Byleistr tried to keep his wits about him and was comforted that Thokk hadn't asked about the boys all evening. The food, unsurprisingly, was salmon. What was surprising, however, was how well it had been cooked. Iárnvidia's cooking was beyond compare. She joked that she'd had plenty of time to practice her culinary skills during the time she'd lived alone. While the husband and wife were talkative, the two sons, Fenrir and Jormungandr, remained quiet for the most part, speaking only when spoken to. Only after his guest was good, drunk, and dumb, did Thokk ask about the blacksmith's wards. Byleistr told Thokk more than he should have, but would not be able to recall saying or being asked anything the following day. Laughter preceded the spinning, and Byleistr soon found himself asking if a bed could be spared as he was in no condition to walk home. Fenrir offered his bed to the guest.

Loki stood outside the house, his hands outstretched toward the fire. He looked younger than his age. His beard was thicker than it once had been, but his hair was still black save for a few grey tufts around his temple. Alongside Angrboda, he had spent the last twenty-four years moving from place to place, never staying in one location for too long, out of fear of being identified. Over the years, Loki had taken on more names than he could remember, Thokk being only the latest in a long line. Everywhere they went, no matter how far or how desolate, Aesir spies were looking for him. He avoided them by being remarkably unremarkable, doing everything in his power to remain out of sight and out of mind.

He hadn't expected to find anything of great interest in Hurrugane. His plan, as always, was to live there for a few months and then move along. Upon walking around the town, he noticed something peculiar: two young men with red hair in the care of the local blacksmith. Loki had always held within himself a deep sense of guilt over leaving Thor broken and alone on the banks of the Iving.

As no news came of Thor's return to Asgard, a profound terror would take Loki as his mind wandered. In his dreams, he would see Thor dead or lost. Then, five years following Baldr's death, news reverberated through the nine realms that the heir had returned home to Asgard safe and sound. *What took him so long?* Loki thought as he heard the news. Although he had his doubts, Loki found his answer in the two red-haired boys.

The door creaked as Angrboda walked out to join her husband.

"A fine meal, Iárnvidia," Loki said. "A meal fit for the king of Jotunheim."

"Fenrir's taken our bed." Angrboda placed her hands on Loki's shoulders. "'You invited him, you deal with him,' is what he said."

Loki laughed. "Stubborn as always." He tapped her hand away and began to pace. Although drunk, he held himself like a sober man. His mind turned toward the men in the forest. Weeks ago, as he and Jormungandr had walked the surrounding area, they spotted a band of men dressed in a garb no one but Loki would have recognized: Aesir garb. Loki had been about to run, but it was too late. They'd seen him, and he could see it in their eyes. They knew who he was. Yet, they did not approach him. Against his best judgment, he decided to walk up to them and speak to them.

Unlike the ones they had come across before, these Aesir were not searching for him. They remained in the shadows, pouncing only when needed. They defended the town's borders from all who would seek to do it harm. Loki was surprised to find out that they were not working on behalf of Odin. In fact, Odin had no idea they were even there. Rather, they were a secret troop working under Thor's orders, unknown to all, and reporting only to him. Loki asked them why they were there, why Thor had placed such importance on protecting this one particular village. The troops had then told him that he'd best be on his way. After seeing the two boys with red hair, it all made sense to him, while also raising several other questions.

"Thor has two Jotunn sons," Loki said, still pacing. "Magni and Modi, the blacksmith's wards. That's why he's protecting this town."

Angrboda let out a deep sigh. "And now I know why we have a stranger sleeping in our son's bed." She looked upwards toward the star-filled sky, then lowered her head to the ground as the thought came upon her. "Never mind," she said.

"What is it?" Loki asked.

"Nothing," Angrboda said. "Never mind, forget it."

"Tell me."

"We've been running for more than twenty years. I don't mind. I'm not complaining. I love you, and being on the run comes with the package. I get that. But what about them? Fenrir and Jormungandr, they've never had a normal life. From one place to another, one place to another. But if we—" She stopped herself. "No, I can't even say it. It's wrong."

"You can say anything to me. I won't judge you."

Angrboda closed her eyes in shame as she allowed the words to slip out. "What if we turn them in, give them to Odin?"

"You think he'll stop coming after us if we do that?" Although Loki tried, he couldn't hide the outrage in his voice.

"He'll see you aren't a threat."

"He bloody well knows I'm not a threat. If I wanted to be king of Jotunheim, I would've bloody well declared myself by now. He knows that. No, this isn't about power or politics or Asgard. This is personal. I killed his son. That's why he wants me." His voice then softened. "We're done running. As long as Thor's sons are here, we're safe. Those boys inside, they'll be able to live a normal life. I'll tear this place down, build us something in town. We'll find each of them a woman. They can settle down." He wrapped his arms around his wife. "It's all going to be alright. I promise. Remember what I told you all those years ago—Thor's the only man I'd trust with my life. I trust him to protect this town. No more running." He gave her a gentle kiss on the cheek. "I promise."

———

Although he hadn't grown out of the habit of calling them boys, Loki knew his sons hadn't been boys in a long time. Jormungandr, the eldest, was nineteen. Fenrir, the hotter-headed of the two, was only ten months younger. By the age of twelve, both of them towered over their father. Despite this, they feared him. It was not a fear born of rage or ill-temper; quite the opposite. Loki never raised his voice or his hand. It was a fear born of reverence. They saw in their father all the qualities they wished to possess: wisdom, cunning, patience. Angrboda, on the other hand, would unleash a fury of screams if one of the two were to misbehave. This they had gotten used to. Loki, however, would sit beside them and ask them to recount why running out of sight, or going hunting unaccompanied, or bringing home a stray dog, was not a good idea. "Every misdeed is a chance to learn. You're not getting up until you tell me what you have learned," he would say to them.

Loki was proud of his sons but lamented that, with no books, parchment, or ink, he could not teach them to read or write. Jotunheim was nothing less than an intellectual desert. Loki often found himself starved for words on a page, but never made this feeling known to anyone but himself. Despite it all—all of the hardships, all of the sleepless nights, the weeks on end they went without food—Loki had found in Jotunheim something he'd never had growing up in Asgard: happiness.

In his family, he found a joy no treasure could bring. This was his reward, he believed. After all, there was no war. The Aesir did not march into Jotunheim, burning and killing every creature that crossed their path. His actions had saved thousands from a senseless and useless death. And no one would ever know, and he would have it no other way. For the most part, his conscience remained clear. Save for one singular weight.

He tried to blot them out, but every now and again, the thought of them came back to him. Angrboda was not his only wife. Fenrir and Jormungandr were not his only sons. His thoughts turned toward Sigyn and Nari. What had come of them? Had Sigyn remarried? What sort of a man did Nari grow up to be? Were they safe? Had Odin—No. Such a thought, he couldn't complete. He had long decided that he would never know, and so he sunk them in the oceans of his mind, forcing them farther down every time until their memory was nothing more than ash in his mouth.

Byleistr awoke the next morning with a throbbing headache, to the hissing sound of eggs sizzling on the pan. He looked out the window. The sun was up. *Late, late, late.* He asked Loki what day of the week it was, and was told it was Wednesday. A sweat took him, and within moments he was out the door, leaving his degmal sitting on the table.

The two boys in his ward had brought him great fortune. They had been delivered to his doorstep when the eldest was eight and the youngest was six. Their mother had been killed in a raid, and no one knew who or where their father was. For the cost of protecting and raising them, Byleistr received a weekly payment—a handful of gold delivered by the man in the hood. Byleistr did not know who the man was or who he was working for, and he didn't care. These were the same men that protected Hurrugane. Therefore, he rationalized, by taking the money and not asking questions he was doing a public service.

Byleistr never saw the man's face. The hood only exposed the bottom of the man's hairy chin. Deep in the forest, the hooded man's voice called out to him, "You're late." Byleistr apologized and bowed his head, not knowing if that was a thing to do or not.

"You shaved," Byleistr said to the man. He straightened himself up and rubbed his hands together. "I'll have you know winters are growing colder. Less food, less fishing, fewer clients. I don't wish for the boys' quality of life to deteriorate."

The man in the hood nodded. Without a word, he outstretched his palm. In it was a small cloth wrapped around twelve gold coins. Byleistr counted them, and counted them again, not noticing the knife until it pierced his throat.

Without expression, the man stared as Byleistr fell to his knees, then the ground. "You've outlived your purpose," the man said as he kicked the corpse of what had once been Byleistr in disgust. "It's time for the heirs of Asgard to return home."

CHAPTER TWENTY-SEVEN

HE'S LATE.

Magni paced around the shop, wondering whether he should open up or keep waiting. The last time he'd opened for business before Byleistr arrived, Byleistr chewed him out. "People come here to see me, not you." The words rang out in Magni's ear. But it was mid-morning, and it was the blacksmith's habit to be at the shop before dawn. Magni turned to his brother, who was sprawled on the cush-ioned chair usually reserved for clients with deeper pockets (of which there were few, if any). "Where do you think he's gone?"

"Probably in some drunken stupor," Modi said, stretching his arms out and yawning. "He could've at least told us he'd be late. Would've gotten some more sleep."

"Do you think we should open up?" Magni believed that if the two made the decision together, then maybe Byleistr's rage would dilute.

"Leave it a little longer." Modi proceeded to shut his eyes and sink deeper into the chair. "If he gets here, wake me up."

Another hour or two passed before Magni grew concerned. He'd decided that opening up the smithy would at least quell his worries by keeping his mind busy. However, that wouldn't be the case. They received a single request that morning: old farmer Heimer needed a pair of horseshoes. Magni made an appointment with him to take the horse's measurements that evening, telling Farmer Heimer he needed to stay in the shop as Byleistr was ill.

"Where the blazes do you think he is?" Magni asked his older brother as noon approached. Modi shrugged, pretending he wasn't concerned and pointed out of the store window as someone neared the shop.

"Good morning, boys," the man said. He was dressed in a black silken robe, something both brothers knew no Jotunn could ever afford. "You don't perchance have anything ready, or is everything custom made?"

Recognizing that the man might have deep pockets, Modi pushed his brother to the side. "Usually custom made, sir. We have a few sample pieces here and there. Maybe we have what you're looking for ready. If we don't, you bet we'll make it for you faster than you can say 'lemon on a stick.' Without sacrificing quality, of course. This here establishment has a reputation to uphold. Finest smithy in the realm. What are you looking for, my good sir?"

The man rubbed his chin. "Sword."

"We've got plenty of those," Modi said. "I'll be right back." Within moments, he was back at the storefront, carrying a selection of weapons, some tall, some short.

The man picked up the blade closest to him. "Sharp," he said as he passed his fingers across the edge. He swung it around. "Well balanced." He placed the sword back on the table. "A fine piece of workmanship. If I may enquire, who forged this beauty?"

"That'll be me, sir," Modi said, standing behind his brother.

"Hmm, and for how much are you willing to part with it? Twelve golden coins?" The man pulled out a small sack and placed it on the table.

The brothers looked at each other. "Done," they said in unison.

The man nodded. "It is a deal. An honest price, honest workmanship. What you told me is true; this just might be the finest smithy in all of Jotunheim." The man turned back just as he was about to walk away. "I didn't get your names."

"I'm Modi. This here's my younger brother Magni."

"Interesting names," said the man. And without another word, he left.

"Well, that was an easy sell," Modi said. "Bet Byleistr will be best pleased when he's back."

"I bet he will be," Magni replied.

There were no more customers that day. It didn't matter. The man in the black hooded cloak had given them more than three times the weapon's asking price, meaning that they had more than met their quota for the day, for the week even. Evening approached.

"Where's that blasted fool?" Modi said. "It'll be dark soon."

"You think we should go look for him?" Magni said.

Modi grunted. "Might as well." He was about to tell his brother that he didn't think they would have another customer today but stopped dead in his tracks as he noticed the rising plume of smoke. Within seconds, they could hear screaming.

Magni turned to his brother. "Close up. Stay here. I'm going to see what it is. Maybe someone needs help."

"Screw the shop. I'm coming," Modi replied.

A horse ran past them. It was old Farmer Heimer's horse. The men came from all sides, breaking whatever they could find. An elderly woman ran out protesting as one of the men entered her shop. She was rewarded with a sword to the throat. The arrows began to rain down, carrying with them a fire that encircled the entire town.

Modi coughed as he ran aimlessly. He felt a large hand on his shoulder. "Get your blasted hands off of me!" he yelled. With all his might, he threw a fist. It landed, breaking the soldier's nose. The soldier placed his hand on the sword's handle. As he was about to unsheathe it, a rock hit him in the back of the head. The soldier turned around to see who it was, giving Modi the chance to kick one of his knee caps out. The man landed on the floor with a thud, letting out a blood-curdling cry.

Farmer Heimer appeared from out of the smoke, riding his horse-driven carriage, ax dripping in his hand. "Not twice in one lifetime!"

"What the hell is going on?" Modi said.

"We're under attack," replied the farmer.

"By who?"

"Bloody Aesir."

As if called forth by a depraved siren, the Aesir troops killed without remorse or emotion. In their path, they spared no man, woman, or child. They numbered more than a hundred. While the youth of the town found fear locked in their hearts, the old, those who remembered the war, found a rage inside of themselves. With sticks, and stones, and bats, and pots, and pans, and any object, blunt or sharp, they fought.

Modi ran back to the shop, hurryingly looking for his weapon of choice—a war hammer. For but a moment he paused, knowing that today he would have to kill or be killed. Steadying his breath, his mind turned toward his training. Byleistr, for all his faults, had at least taught him how to fight, and today he would put that training to use. He charged. The hammer found its target more often than it missed.

Coughing under the broken wall, Magni cried for help. From all sides, they surrounded him, picking up the stones that covered his body. He waited for it, the blade that would end it all, but it never came. They began to tie his hands. Then, a shrill yell, one that Magni recognized, came forth. The soldiers stepped out of the way as Modi attacked. "Get away from my little brother, you bastards!" Grabbing the opportunity, Magni leaped at one of the men, pulling him down with the rope and taking his sword away from him. The soldier stood in place, as if he was allowing Magni to cut him down.

He looked up. From every direction they came. The brothers stood back to back. Modi readied his hammer. Magni brandished the sword. The archers drew, and the man in black, the same one they had sold a sword to earlier that day, emerged from between them. "My sires, your grandfather calls you home. Lay down your arms and come peacefully. Fail to do so, and you will be taken by force."

The words passed by them. Without thinking, the brothers attacked. A string of arrows flew toward them, aimed with careful precision. Magni was struck in the shoulder while Modi dropped to the floor as the projectiles bore through his thigh. The brothers lay incapacitated. The soldiers walked forward, rope in hand.

Modi tried to lift himself. He screamed as his legs buckled. He gripped his hammer and looked toward his brother. Blood dripped down Magni's shoulder as he pulled the arrow out. He pulled himself up, only to have his feet kicked out from underneath him. The rope burned as they wrapped it tightly around his wrists. "Let go of him," cried Modi, writhing. He gripped the hammer as tightly as he could. If he was to be taken, he thought, he wouldn't make it easy for them. A boot landed on his skull as soon as the thought came, replacing pain and courage with a black emptiness.

The fire surrounded them in a haze of black smoke, blocking the surrounding area from view. The clashing of swords echoed through Magni's ears. Through the veil of dark and flame, he could hear voices. Voices he knew. Jotunn voices. Not cowering but angry. A bloodied Aesir soldier emerged from the smoldering gloom, a rake—a tool used to scrape fallen leaves together—driven through his chest. Small pools of red encircled the areas where the teeth had pierced his flesh. He fell to his knees as the rider behind him approached. The rider was not a soldier, a wired machine purpose-built for war. It was an old woman, no younger than sixty, riding a donkey. "Not again, you pigs," she said, cutting off the soldier's head with a butcher's knife in one swift motion.

The Aesir primed their weapons to attack, but before they could move a muscle, the horde arrived. A constant wave of fighters. Not soldiers. Fighters. Ordinary men, women, and even a few children, old and young, driven by something altogether beautiful and dreadful, to defend their land from all those who would wish to do it harm. On horses, donkeys, and mules, they sped through the Aesir, striking in every direction with shovels, rakes, knives, ropes, sickles, bars of metal, rocks, and anything that had the potential to hurt.

Modi tried to raise himself amid the chaos. The leg was no good, not working. Every moment was more painful than the one that came before it, driving him down. He crawled toward his brother, rolling out of the way as horse hooves blasted dirt into his eyes. Wiping his face, he continued until he was at his brother's side. He slapped Magni's face gently. "Wake up. Wake up." Magni's eyes squinted open before widening at the sight before him. *They're falling back*, he thought, not believing his eyes.

"I can't walk," said Modi, pointing to the wound. Magni pulled himself upright. His head spun. He nearly keeled over, but stopped himself. He leaned down, grabbed Modi's arm, and thrust it upward and around his shoulder. They were surrounded from every side, not by Aesir, but by those that had come to defend them.

The soldiers started to run, terror filling every iota of their being. The townsfolk chased them, pelting them with stones. "After 'em!" Farmer Heimer roared. As the Aesir sprinted in the smoky darkness of their own creation, they were cut down, all of them, one by one.

CHAPTER TWENTY-EIGHT

"WE NEED TO GO," Loki said, slamming the front door behind himself. "Take what you need. Leave everything else behind. Quickly."

"What's going on?" Angrboda said, before looking out the window. Smoke covered the cloudless blue sky in a grey haze. She placed her hand to her lips. "No, no, no, not again." She began to take shallow, rapid breaths. "We need to help them," she said as she ran toward the cupboard. The sword was heavy in her arms. It had been years since she'd lifted it.

"We have to go," said Loki once more, rushing around the small house in a frenzy. "Where are the boys?"

"Not again. Not again. Not again." Angrboda's panic took over her.

"Where are the boys?"

She caught herself for a moment. "The river. They went to the river. They're on the boat."

Loki knelt and gripped his wife's hands as firmly as he could. "We need to find the boys and get out of here." He looked up, out the window, toward the smoke. "We can't do anything to help them." He wiped the tears falling down her cheeks. "I need you to be strong. We have to find the boys and leave."

Angrboda ceased panting. "We have to leave. We have to keep the boys safe," she repeated.

"Come on," Loki said, holding her hand, slowly guiding her out of the front door.

It was as if it had materialized from nothing, a lone messenger of death hurtling through the air from oblivion. The arrow pierced her throat as soon as she stepped outside. She fell with a thud, dead before her body hit the ground. Loki dropped to his knees.

It was as if everything that existed ceased to be, a fire made of darkness enveloping the universe. He called her name and shook her, but no answer came. He closed his eyes and opened them, hoping that this was some demon-inspired nightmare. "Don't leave me," he said. Tears fell. "Please, don't go. Come back to me." He looked around and saw them. A voice in the back of his mind called him to run, to get away, to find his sons and leave this cursed place. Just as he was about to stand, a force from within held him in place, paralyzing him in his grief, whispering to him that death might be the sweetest reprieve. Then, he heard their voices.

Fenrir and Jormungandr rushed to his side. A shudder took them as they looked upon their grief-stricken father and their mother's dead body. *Grief can wait*, thought Fenrir as the men drew closer. He outstretched his palm to Loki. "Father, we have to run away."

"Go!" Loki barked. "I'm not leaving her." He stopped himself before he could say it. *Let them have me.* Seeing the expression on their faces, he steadied himself, kissed Angrboda's forehead, and stood up, her sword in one hand and his bow in the other. He drew an arrow and took careful aim. The shot made its mark. He took a deep breath. "Run," he told his sons. "I'll cover you." The enemy's arrow, in return, landed by Loki's feet. A warning shot. He recognized the markings and the make of the projectile. "It's me they're after." Fenrir and Jormungandr stood in place. "Go," he said, in a manner close to pleading.

Fenrir darted into the house, and within moments was out again. He threw Jormungandr one of the two blades he was holding. "Those bastards killed my mother," he said as the sword danced in front of him. "I'm going to kill every single one of them." His eyes were red, but he did not allow himself to cry.

What had been but black specks in the distance now took the shapes of men, far closer, armed and armored. "If you love me," Loki said, "you'll run." Fenrir raised his weapon. "Run!" Loki said in a biting tone his sons had never heard before. Fenrir lowered his arm, a look of defeat painted on his face. Loki grabbed a handful of arrows. He scanned the perimeter and began to count. *One. Two. Three. Four. Five. Six. Seven.* The arrows flew in quick succession, but however many of the enemy fell, many more remained. He could hear his sons' footsteps. At first loud, but within moments a distant echo. He drew once more and fired.

The enemy's arrows came from all sides, making contact with nothing but the ground. The men were close enough to shoot him, but while Loki scarcely missed a shot, the Aesir appeared to be purposefully missing him. They fired up and beyond him, away toward the river. It then dawned on him, a stark realization he would have had far earlier had he not been so engulfed in his grief. Odin's words all those years ago filled his mind. "I share with you my blood, Loki, that we may be brothers, and you an adopted son to my father, and swear never to harm you." He repeated them once more in his head. "... *And swear never to harm you.*" A weight fleetingly hung around Loki as he grasped that such an oath did not extend to Jormungandr and Fenrir.

The Aesir covered the banks of the river. The burnt shards of what had been Loki's boat drifted down the waterway, carried by the roaring currents. Fenrir took a step backward, closing the gap between himself and his brother. "Nowhere to go, young one," said one of the Aesir. "You're trapped."

Loki called to them but could not stop it. Outnumbered and with no other option, Jormungandr grabbed his brother by the shoulder and pulled him into the water. "Good for them," said the soldier. "Better to die freezing but free than to die warm and in chains. An honorable exit." He turned to Loki. "Same can't be said for you. The king, he's got plans for you. Special plans. Royal plans. Plans that'll—" The arrow pierced his left lung and the other his right eye socket.

Three arrows left. Loki unsheathed the sword, waiting for the Aesir to attack. They did no such thing. They stood in place, motionless and without expression. Not allowing himself to feel, to think of anything, to focus on anything but killing as many as he possibly could, Loki swung the sword. It pierced the soldier's heavy armor at the shoulder, but not the flesh beneath. Loki pulled, but the blade was stuck. The soldier grabbed Loki by the throat, careful not to squeeze too hard as not to leave a mark, and lifted him, before dropping him to the ground.

The silk rope was soft and gentle to the touch. "Careful," said the soldier as Loki writhed in his bonds, "you don't want to hurt yourself."

CHAPTER TWENTY-NINE

THE CURRENT WAS STRONG, pulling Fenrir in every direction. His body crashed upon the rocks. He tried to hold on to something, anything, but the sheer force of the tide heaved him away. It dragged him under, and when he felt as though his lungs would finally give out, it pushed him up. He outstretched his arms, begging for a rock or branch to grab onto.

The hands pulled him by the shirt and by his hair. He coughed, touching the dry soil, and looked up to see his brother. Though the better swimmer, Jormungandr wasn't much less worse for wear. He shivered. The waters were cold, but not cold enough to freeze.

"Wood," Jormungandr said. "Fire. Warm. We need to get warm. Or die. Die. Die of cold. Warm now. Up. Before too cold."

Fenrir struggled to stand. His teeth chattered too vigorously to allow him to speak. Years ago, their mother had taught them how to start a fire with sticks, but it was something they hadn't had to do in a very long time. Jormungandr searched his mind for the instructions, blocking out the pain, the cold, and the grief. *Fine tinder. Finer is better.* He looked for his sword in his delirium, forgetting that he'd dropped it in the river to stop himself from sinking. "Sword. Sword. Where sword. Sword cut. Need sword. Fire. Fire need cut. Cut wood. Fire. Warm."

"Walk," Fenrir finally managed. "No fire. Walk. Hurrugane. We go, Hurrugane. Hurrugane fire." He pointed to the grey cloud emanating from a place not too far from their location.

Jormungandr grunted. "Hurrugane danger. It's danger. Dangerous. We can't. We cannot. Attack. We can't go there. It's under attack." The shivering began to subside just enough to allow his speech to start to return to normal.

"No choice," replied Fenrir. "Too weak. We're too weak. Make fire." He clenched his fists as if he wished to warm himself through pure strength of will. "We need to go back to Hurrugane. We'll die of cold out here."

Jormungandr nodded reluctantly.

Though the walk was not long, it was merciless. Every step seemed like a mile. Every breath grew heavier than the one before it. The wind whipped their damp clothing, cutting through them, a torture not unlike being stabbed by a thousand small shards of glass.

It was night by the time they reached what had once been the town of Hurrugane. A putrid stench emanated from a large fire on the outskirts. Fenrir and Jormungandr ran to it, the attraction to its warmth outweighing their disgust at the miasma. Human bodies fueled the flame, an untold number, perhaps a hundred. Fear and loathing filled the brothers, but as they were about to run, they noticed the armor. The burning bodies were Aesir.

They ventured deeper. It was as if a storm had come, breaking brick and wood and steel. Everything lay in ruin, not a single building unharmed. A quiet lingered in the air. A silence cut only by the faraway rumbling. They walked toward the town hall. Light emanated from within. Their pace quickened. Light was good. Light meant people.

"What are you two doing outside?" said an old croaky voice just as they were about to enter.

"Why are you out here?" said Jormungandr to the old man.

"I asked you first," the old man groused. Jormungandr stared back, his expression blank. "Keeping watch, just in case there's more of those blasted buggers."

"What's happening in there?"

"Questions. They're prodding the survivor. Eventually, they'll—" He dragged his finger across his neck. "—but before that, they'll pull everything they can out of him. I just want to know if we're at war again. One war's enough for one lifetime. Go on then. Everyone's inside. Get out of the cold."

As was often the case in Jotunheim, Hurrugane's town elders were a fickle bunch. Their indecision was often covered by a mask of feigned wisdom, the sort of wisdom usually attributed to those with stern expressions and long white beards. Lyfinder, the oldest (but least senile) of the elders walked back and forth as he spoke. "Are we at war?" The Aesir laughed in response. If the laughter bothered Lyfinder, he certainly did not show it. Thrusting the fireplace poker through the Aesir's foot he once more said, "Are we at war?" just as calmly as he had the first time. He pulled back the poker, which took with it flesh and bone.

The Aesir bit his tongue, resisting every urge to howl, but he could not contain himself when the poker struck him in the face. "You're asking the wrong questions, old man." He spat on the floor a tooth bathed in dark red. "Kill me and be done with it; you've got naught to threaten me with." And with that, he continued to laugh to himself.

A cold stillness enveloped the hall, broken only by the loud creaking of a door in dire need of oiling. Seeing the smile on the Aesir's face, Fenrir could not contain himself. He marched forward, snatched the poker from the old man's hand, thrust it through the Aesir's knee cap, and began to twist. An uncontainable scream burst forth from the Aesir. Fenrir grabbed him by the hair. "Where did they take him? Tell me, and I'll end it fast. Don't, and you will beg me for death's sweet embrace. Where have they taken him?" *Taken who?*

wondered the crowd. As far as they were aware, no one had been taken from the village.

The Aesir forced out a laugh. "We didn't get Thor's bastards, but at least we got your great king. Long live Loki of Jotunheim." Fenrir drove the poker, which was still lodged between the Aesir's shattered bones, upwards. Along with the wail came a mouthful of blood. *Long live the king? Loki of Jotunheim?* The crowd's minds began to wander. *Could it be?* Some began to connect the dots.

Fenrir wiped his face. "Where are they taking him? Where are they taking my father?"

"Odin's got something special in store for him."

Fenrir pulled the poker backward, and before Jormungandr could interject, drove it through the Aesir's throat.

Lyfinder walked forward. "Loki of Jotunheim," he mumbled to himself. "Farbauti's son. Heir to the throne. Surely it cannot be." He raised his head to face Fenrir. "Thokk. You're Thokk's boys. Not under my nose. He cannot be. After all these years." The old man's welled up. "My son, your father's name is Thokk, is it not?"

He wouldn't want this, Jormungandr thought as Fenrir walked forward. "My father's name?" Fenrir said, looking to his brother, searching for approval. Jormungandr nodded halfheartedly. "My father is Loki Laufeyson, son of Farbauti, the rightful king of Jotunheim."

"My princes!" Lyfinder fell to his knees, his eyes moist and red. The crowd followed suit. "For years, we've prayed for it, and it is here —Farbauti's line, reborn. I offer you my servitude, swearing on pain of death, and on the deaths of my grandchildren, I will help you save your father. I will help you save our king!"

CHAPTER THIRTY

THE CARRIAGE ROCKED to and fro, shaking Loki into consciousness. The interior of the carriage was lined with gold; its seats were wide and upholstered with fine linen. It had a cupboard with a deceptively small glass door, stocked with anything a man on a long journey would need to make himself comfortable. Loki rubbed his wrists. They weren't sore, to his surprise. He stared out the window. Hurrugane was now many miles away, he knew. Beside the carriage, in front of it, and behind it, the soldiers rode, protecting their valuable cargo.

Loki steadied himself, his head still rushing. Then, in an instant, it all came back to him. Angrboda. Jormungandr. Fenrir. The river's current was strong, he remembered, strong enough to sink the mightiest of men. He postulated the likeliness of their survival for a moment, letting out a raging shriek, followed by a whimper.

His eyes traced the cupboard. In it, he could see through the glass door, was dried meat, packed in a way as to hide the smell; and wine, many bottles of wine, enough to keep a man drunk for months on end. He opened the door, grabbed a bottle, smelled it, and began to drink. He did not drink to remember or to forget. He drank to leave. Leave his mind completely, leave the shell of what had once been Loki to waste away, and bask in the glow of thoughtless inebriation.

And as he drank, he grew angry, and as he grew angry, he grew violent—a useless violence directed at everything, including himself. "Cowards, the lot of you," he said to the coachman. "The brave and mighty soldiers of Asgard, killing women and boys." He took another swig and stood up, his knees wobbling as the carriage shook. "Go on, finish it." The coachman did not react. "How did it feel? How did it feel as I stuck your men, your brothers, full of arrows? Did you bury them? Or did you leave them for the buzzards to pick clean?"

It was as if Loki's voice carried no weight, plunging into silence the moment it left his throat. Nothing came. Not a single remark. Not a laugh. Not a snide comment or a threat. Loki sunk back into his seat, gripping the bottle as though it held the elixir of life. Sleep did not come, nor did waking—nothing but their haunting glow. "Everything," he said to himself as the night blotted all from sight. "Everything. You took everything." It was a whimper. "Just kill me. Please." He opened the small carriage window, stuck his head outside, and screamed into the darkness, before being sick all over the carriage's door.

Loki whispered to himself as the days passed. In his mind, he replayed the only scene that brought him back any semblance of sanity. He envisioned Odin, on the floor, laying in a pool of his own blood. Loki salivated as he imagined plunging in a short blade, one that would not kill, but inflict so much pain upon him as to make him crave death. As the carriage moved, day in and day out, the delusion grew stronger. In his mind, he saw increasingly depraved methods of torture, ones that do not bear repeating in this text.

Rocked between drunkenness and fantasy, he was oblivious as days passed without him even knowing what he once had been. The man who had stopped a war and saved thousands of lives vanished, replaced by a creature swimming in its own misery. He asked for death multiple times a day, hoping beyond hope that one soldier would, at long last, grow fed up with his incessant nagging and finish him once and for all. They never so much as acknowledged him; the sound of his screams faded into the void as soon as he spoke them.

CHAPTER THIRTY-ONE

It was a simple grave, without a name, or indeed any identifying features. Jormungandr and Fenrir stood beside it, looking on to the burial of the dead. "Too many," Jormungandr said so quietly that no one heard him. Though victorious, the people of Hurrugane had no joy in their victory. How could they? This was not a battle, and these were not soldiers. No great speeches were made in the name of courage and valiance. Instead, sons spoke of their love of their mothers, wives spoke of the kindness of their husbands, and fathers spoke of the gentleness of their daughters. All of them gone, never to come back, murdered for nothing but malice and the dull lure of power.

Fenrir's head hung low. Her voice rang through his head; he could hear it as clearly as he could hear the blowing wind. He could see all of it—the lessons she taught him, the times he lay in her lap while she brushed his hair, the times she'd hug him and give him a small peck on the cheek. He was supposed to say something, anything, but it did not come. Words failed. How could words, mere words, convey her? She was more than he could describe. Try as he might, he would never be able to do her justice. Perhaps an injustice might suffice, Fenrir thought, but still he could not bear it.

"A light in an endless cascade of grey, that was what my mother was," Jormungandr said. "When times were hard, and food grew scarce, she never gave in to fear or complained, always telling us to hold on to hope. When I was a boy, she carried me, sang to me. And as I grew up, and when she could no longer carry me, she still sang. If I had trouble sleeping, she'd sit by the door and sing. What good is in me, I owe to her. She showed me patience, forbearance, courage. She taught me how to fight, how to use a sword. She taught me how to climb, to track, to hunt. But most of all, she showed me what it means to love and be loved unconditionally. Whatever I say, however much I tell you about her, I can't hope to show you anything but a fraction of what she was." He stepped back as if to announce that that was all he could bear to say.

The burials continued until night came. Some returned home, taking with them many of those whose houses had been burned down. Most, however, went back to the town hall. The elders sat huddled together in a corner. They spoke in whispers, passing between them a small piece of parchment. They critiqued the words written on it. The words had to be right, to convey the sheer joy while also not overshadowing the terrible events that had befallen their town. Only once Lyfinder deemed the words to his liking did they make their move.

Jormungandr and Fenrir sat alone by a fire, one of the numerous fires inside the hall. It was a bitterly cold night, and most did not have coats thick enough. With stern conviction, Lyfinder walked over to them and handed them the parchment.

"What's this?" Fenrir said.

"Well, read it," Lyfinder replied with the giddiness of a child.

"I can't read." Fenrir patted Jormungandr's knee. "Neither can he. Read it to us."

Lyfinder puffed his chest. "This is addressed to the elders of Jotunheim. 'I write to you with both sorrow and joy in my heart. Information has come to light of extreme importance to the realm's wellbeing. Hurrugane has come under Aesir attack. Though hard fought, we proved to be the battle's victor, though many fell. Following the battle, it came to our attention that Farbauti's line lives. Loki Laufeyson, son of Farbauti, the rightful king of Jotunheim, lives. The enemy has captured him. For more than forty years, Jotunheim has lived in the dark. In the midst of this tragedy, we find light if only we are able to fight for it. Princes Jormungandr and Fenrir, the heirs to the throne, call upon you. Our king is in danger. We ask you to save our king. We ask you to fight for the good of the realm, for the good of Jotunheim.'"

"Not good enough," Fenrir said.

"Sire, what more do you wish me to say? The people of Jotunheim will fight to their deaths for their king. This letter calls on them to do so."

"We will save my father, but that is not all we're going to do," Fenrir said. "I have spent my entire life running from Odin. No more. I will rip him out, root and stem. I will tear down his castle, brick by brick. I will rain down hell on Asgard. I am Odin's deeds incarnate. I will burn his house to the ground, and only after he's seen everything and everyone he loves die will I kill him. Odin will face the fury of Jotunheim. Write that."

CHAPTER THIRTY-TWO

WITH A LOUD THUD, his head smashed into the cupboard's door. He rubbed his temple but saw no red. *Lucky*, Loki thought in his moment of hungover half-sobriety. Having spent the better part of six weeks being rocked back and forth, the stillness was loathsome. *We've stopped.* Throwing himself backward and up onto the chair, he looked outside. The realization shook him. In his drunkenness, he'd missed Midgard. Winters, growing colder and more bitter with every year, transformed Asgard's landscape into something Loki vaguely recognized. A land that had never seen snow in his lifetime was now coated in white. Blue skies, for the first time in over a century, became grey and silver. The trees, which, in previous times, shone gold in the winter, were now brown and leafless. The carriage's door squealed as it swung open.

He had dark circles under his eyes. His once auburn hair was now, with the exception of a few tufts, completely grey, aging him far beyond his years. Though just as tall, he was not as broad as he once had been. Loki could see the years had not been kind to him, but despite the drastic change in his appearance, Loki could never mistake him for someone else. Thor climbed aboard, careful to not step on the shards of glass spread on the carpeted floor as he sat down.

"You look like shit," Loki said, letting a smile slip out.

"So do you," replied Thor. In his younger years, he might've noted the smell, but time and experience had provided him with the facility needed not to say everything that came to mind. "I'm happy to see you, brother. I just wish it would've been under different circumstances. I am truly sorry for your loss."

"You have nothing to apologize for. It was Odin who ordered the attack," Loki said with the sort of conviction he'd almost forgotten he possessed. "I only ask one thing of you. I don't know how, but I ask that when the time comes, you stay out of my way."

"My father is many things. He is capable of violence I can never understand. But he is still my father." He placed a hand on Loki's lap. "I've never been a good liar. And I won't do you the disservice of treating you as a fool."

"He murdered my wife. He murdered my sons. He burnt a town of innocent people to the ground. And he probably murdered your sons." Loki's voice was quiet but hot; dim, but biting. He noticed the stunned expression on Thor's face. "How did I know, you're wondering? I pieced it together. Not completely; I don't know who the mother was, and I have no idea how or why they were under the blacksmith's care. But I know it was your men that defended Hurrugane. Care to fill in the blanks?"

And so Thor told him.

Twenty-four years prior, Thor had awoke on the banks of the Iving, his body a bruised wreck. He waited for three days, and then he wandered in the direction of home. Unfortunately, he hadn't the foggiest clue which direction it was. And so, rather than walk toward Asgard, he'd marched right back into Jotunheim. Sleeping in the cold and damp, finding nothing to hunt, it dawned on him: He might die. He lay shivering one night. Despite having not seen a soul for two weeks, it wasn't the cold or hunger that bothered him the most. It was the quiet and the thought of dying alone. The warmth of the fire woke him. He looked to his right. An old man sat beside him. Thor feared being killed in his sleep; opening his eyes and finding a blade rammed down his throat. The old man had no such interest. His moral code compelled him to help all those who need it and all those who seek it. He took Thor in, not caring whether he was a Jotunn or an Aesir. He was a man in need, and that was that.

Although Thor had been far from death, he was in no state to make the journey back home. The old man, an unlucky fisherman called Samsur, told Thor in no uncertain terms, "You may stay in my home for as long as you need. When you are strong and healthy, only then will I allow you to make the journey back."

Samsur lived with his wife, Jordubad, and daughter, Jarnsaxa, in a small cabin in the Jotunn wilderness. The only food they ate was fish from the Iving and, more rarely, lost deer. Thor was immediately taken by the old man's generosity and simplicity, not to mention his ravishingly beautiful daughter. There, Thor found something he'd had no idea he'd ever wanted, something he couldn't put into words: a serenity forcing his hand, changing the course of his life. He asked Samsur if he could stay with them indefinitely. Having tasted the best of luxury, and seeing firsthand what unchecked desire could do to a man, his heart yearned to remain with the simple and the humble. "You pull your weight," Samsur said. "That's my only condition. Lighten my load, and you can stay here for as long as you like." And so he did. If fishing was needed, Thor fished. If hunting was needed, Thor hunted. If supplies needed bringing from afar, Thor went (with a map and some guidance, of course).

Two years passed before he plucked up the courage to ask for Jarnsaxa's hand in marriage. He'd assumed that he'd been declared dead by now, and as such, Sif was no longer his wife. The wedding was a simple affair. They said their vows in the presence of the bride's father and mother.

Jarnsaxa was pregnant by the third year and pregnant again during the fourth. During that time, Thor noticed Aesir troops patrolling the Jotunn banks of the Iving. They were looking for him, and they were looking for Loki, Thor assumed. He stayed out of sight. By the fifth year, the number of Aesir troops in Jotunheim troubled him. Sif was barren, unable to provide Thor—and by extension, Odin—an heir. But now he had two sons . . .two Jotunn sons. Dread permeated his very being. Odin, Thor knew, would never allow a Jotunn to sit on the throne of Asgard. If he was to ever learn about the boys, he would no doubt kill them.

Samsur had always assumed that Thor was nothing more than an Aesir soldier. Thor, on his part, never corrected the assumption. Until that fateful night. "I'm not who you think I am," Thor said. "I am Odin's son, the heir to the throne of Asgard." He left them that night with a heavy heart, promising them that one day he would be back.

Upon his return, Thor had never seen Odin so happy. "My son," were the only words he could muster, repeating them endlessly. In celebration, Odin ordered the slaughter of two hundred calves and held a feast unlike any the realm had ever seen before. Within mere months, Thor was reinstated as Master of Arms. Fearing that one day Loki might declare himself, Odin made sure to keep the army, a force five thousand strong, stationed at the castle's walls. Thor got to work getting to know the men, finding those he might trust.

Fifty men had left with Baldr all those years ago. Only fourteen returned. They informed Odin that Loki had murdered Baldr and only escaped because he was holding a blade to Thor's throat and that any attack would risk the prince's life. Odin had them hung, drawn, and quartered, hanging their heads from the castle walls.

Soon after that, Odin sent troops to Jotunheim to search for Thor and Loki. The old adage "Aesir blood cannot go unavenged" was thrown by the wayside. The troops were told, under no uncertain terms, that if they fell, they would not be avenged. Odin could not risk war. To go to war was to risk his son's life. More than that, if Loki were to be killed in the fighting, he would have betrayed his oath. Thor took a similar approach. Upon finding men he trusted, Thor ordered them to find his sons and keep watch over them.

In the intervening time, however, raiders attacked Samsur's cabin. Thor's troops found the old man's body, as well as that of his wife and daughter—Thor's wife. The boys, on the other hand, were nowhere to be found. The soldiers searched far and wide, eventually finding the raiding party and the boys. They killed the pillagers without impunity and, for a hefty fee, placed the boys in the care of a blacksmith who'd previously been an informant to Asgard, in the town of Hurrugane. They set a perimeter around the town, protecting it from all those who might do it ill, and keeping watch over the boys from a distance.

"Loyalty is a fickle thing," Thor said as Loki listened intently. A man among the troop had grown disillusioned with seeing his brothers fall time and time again, protecting a land that was not theirs, without recompense. He returned back to Asgard and informed Odin of everything. In turn, Odin had him killed and ordered Thor's troops snuffed out.

"I thought that I'd kept them safe. That when I was king, I would bring them here to Asgard, and they would be my successors." Thor looked down at his feet. "I promise you one thing, Loki. I won't let you live in bondage. When the time is right, I will save you. And together, we'll find our boys, bring them back here safe. That I promise you."

Loki rubbed his chin, processing what he'd just heard. "Now," he said. "Free me now. The men outside, you can take them."

"Once, a long time ago, yes. But not now. I have spent fourteen years living in nothing but worry, and it has spent me. As the mind grows weak and weary, the body follows suit."

Loki sunk deeper into his seat. "How's Mimir?"

Thor shook his head. "Age takes the mind and has its terrible ways with it." He paused momentarily. "He began to speak of a coming fire, the end of Asgard. Ragnarok, he called it in his delirium. For years, he begged Odin to abandon Asgard. 'The realm will die,' he would say. 'A burning from below. It will come from Muspelheim.' Odin did what any sane man would do. He ignored such talk. Mimir, seeing no other option, sent letters to the kings of Yggdra, begging them to aid in Asgard's evacuation. Odin loved his counsel, but could not allow him to go on preaching the end of all. Mimir did not fight. He did not beg. He was brave, facing his death with such honor and conviction that I began to doubt he'd even gone mad."

"Swallowed by the earth," Loki said, recalling his final conversation with his teacher. His eyes turned red. "I hope it's true. I hope Asgard burns." He slammed his feet on the floor of the carriage. "Get out."

Thor did so without protest. Loki's eyes turned toward the cabinet. From inside, he produced a bottle, and as his fingers moved to uncork it, he stopped himself. The carriage began to rock back and forth once again. He placed the bottle back into the cupboard.

CHAPTER THIRTY-THREE

THE LETTER READ AS FOLLOWS:

To the elders of Jotunheim,

I write to you with both sorrow and joy in my heart. Hurrugane has come under Aesir attack. Although the battle was won, many fell. Our town lies in ruin. But amid this darkness comes good news. The line of Farbauti lives.

The enemy has taken Loki Laufeyson, the rightful king of Jotunheim. Our king escaped the clutches of the Aesir many years ago. He remained in hiding to avoid war with Asgard and spare innocent blood. His sacrifice was repaid with treachery.

Jotunheim's princes, Fenrir and Jormungandr, call upon you for aid. For too long has Jotunheim lived under the heel. It is now time for action. We ask you to pledge your undying allegiance to them and to march with them into the belly of the beast. Asgard must pay for what it has done.

Now is the time for reckoning.

Regards,

Lyfinder Haakenson

They sat in anticipation for three weeks, but nothing came. The townsfolk began to talk, saying that no one believed the claim, or perhaps Jotunheim was in such chaos and desperation that no one could afford to come or send word. By the fourth week, everything changed. An unending flurry of ravens and messengers came from far and wide to bring the good news. "Long live the line of Farbauti," some wrote, while others made their intentions known more clearly: "We'll carry Odin's head to your doorstep, and you, my princes, can have the honor of pissing on it." By the fifth week, Fenrir and Jormungandr had a force of over a thousand under their command, with five thousand more on the way.

The events of the previous month weighed down upon Jormungandr's mind. "Father wouldn't want this," he told himself, swatting the thought away as fast as it came. Instead, he busied himself with the creation of a code of conduct for the army. "We will pass by no towns and villages. No harm shall come to the people of Asgard, only those deemed guilty." Some took issue with this philosophy, stating that Asgard had never provided them with such mercy. "We will not return evil, like for like. We are better than that. We will teach them what it means to wage war with honor and dignity."

By the sixth week, word went out, informing all those answering the call to meet the army by the Iving. The brothers did not wish to inconvenience the people of Midgard. Winters, growing fiercer by the year, replaced the Little Sea's water with thick layers of ice. News came that Asgard had increased its military presence within the area. "Good," Fenrir said upon hearing the news. "We can give them a taste of our might."

One night, as the army camped, Fenrir's thoughts turned toward the only secret left to be told. "We tell them tonight," he told his brother. "It's their right to know." Jormungandr had hoped to avoid this, believing that informing Magni and Modi of their lineage might dissuade them from attacking Asgard. After all, they might be forced to kill their own father. He reluctantly agreed and sent for them.

"You're wondering why we called you here," Fenrir said. "I was informed that when the Aesir attacked Hurrugane, they had every opportunity to kill both of you and yet did not. Instead, they attempted to capture you. Do you know why?"

The brothers shook their heads in unison.

"Who is your father?" Jormungandr said.

"Our parents were killed when we were children," Magni said. "We have no memory of them, sire."

"It is not befitting for a prince to call another sire," Fenrir said, a coy smile sneaking toward the edge of his lip.

Magni stood perplexed, unlike his brother, unable to discern what was meant.

"Perhaps you noticed my father's interest in you," Fenrir said. Modi nodded. "Did you ever ask yourself why that might be?"

"Not many gingers in Jotunheim," Magni said. "At least that's why most people look at us funny."

"'Your grandfather calls you home,'" Modi said. "The Aesir who attacked us, that's what he said. 'Your grandfather calls you home.'" He looked Fenrir in the eye. "The Aesir we questioned after the battle, he said they hadn't caught 'Thor's bastards.'" He took a step back. "It can't be, can it?"

Fenrir nodded. "You are not bastards," he said. "You are the legitimate sons of Thor Odinson, Prince of Asgard. Which one of you is the older?"

It was as if an invisible man had entered the room, striking Magni across the face. He stared blankly at his brother, almost forgetting to blink.

"Speak up then."

"Me," said Modi. "I'm the older one."

Jormungandr placed his hand on Modi's shoulder. "Then you are the heir to the throne of Asgard. When this war is finished, you will be king of Asgard."

Magni blinked uncontrollably before bursting into ecstatic laughter. "You can't be serious!" Fenrir and Jormungandr did not flinch. "By the gods, you're actually serious." He turned to his brother. "Slap me."

"What?" Modi said.

"I'm dreaming. Slap me, so I wake up."

Before Modi could even move, Fenrir wrapped his palm across Magni's face.

"That settles it. I'm not dreaming," Magni said, lifting his hand to his cheek.

"No, you're not," said Fenrir.

Modi raised his hand, not unlike a schoolboy. "Does this mean he has to call me sire?" He pointed at Magni.

Magni's eyes widened. "Piss off!"

CHAPTER THIRTY-FOUR

WITH ITS TOWERING GREY WALLS, stained glass windows, and spiraling towers, the castle was a figure frozen in time. The door screeched as it flung open. Loki trembled as he stepped down. The harsh weather had wilted every plant in the garden. Beyond the rust-covered gate stood the Aesir king.

"Good to see you, brother," Odin said, walking toward the carriage. "It's been far too long. You had us all worried. I hope your journey went smoothly." He pulled Loki in close and hugged him. "I can't tell you how much I've missed you. Where are my manners? You must be tired." He sniffed. "I'll have them draw you a bath. Tonight we eat, and we toast, and we get roaring drunk. You must tell me how you've been keeping. But not yet. That is a conversation fitting only of a feast."

He walked Loki to the bath. It was a long walk. Odin did not leave a moment empty of talk for its entire duration. Loki saw nothing but red and heard nothing but rage. Background noise was all it was, vile and empty background noise. The water was hot, almost too hot, as Loki got in. A shaving blade was left on the edge of the tub. Loki stared at it, and then at his wrists. *End it,* called a voice in the back of his mind. *End it now.* He brushed it away.

Loki had never seen the hall empty. Although food covered every table, enough to feed a village, no one was there. No one but Odin. He sat at the head of the largest table, in his customary seat. "Come, brother, come. Let us dine and let us drink." Loki sat beside him. "Tell me, Loki, what have you been doing all of these many years?" Although his voice was calm, madness dwelled in Odin's eyes. "Talk to me, brother. Say something." Loki remained quiet. "Have it your way." Odin tore the leg off a chicken. "Go on, eat." Loki didn't move a muscle. "No, no, perhaps it's not food you're after. Drink. That is what you seek." He looked toward the servant standing by the door. "Mead!"

Two tankards came. The liquid dribbled down Odin's beard. "Drink, brother." Loki remained frozen. "You don't want to eat. You don't want to drink. What do you want? Name it, and it's yours. Your blood runs through my veins. Anything your heart desires, name it and you'll have it."

Loki slammed his fists on the table. "Why don't you just be done with it and kill me?"

Odin rubbed his beard. "An oath is an oath, brother. I swore to my father that I would never harm you." He pushed the chair back and stood. "Do you know what the difference between an oath and a promise is? A promise is a vow made to another person to do or not do something. Easy to make and easy to break. But an oath—that is a vow made in the presence of the gods. It is a thing unto itself holy and sacred. To break an oath is to lie to the gods. Loki, you have put me in a predicament. I would love nothing more than to kill you." He took a sip of his drink. "But not before unleashing upon you every method of torture that springs to my mind. Unfortunately, I have sworn an oath not to do so. You killed my son. You turned my other son and heir against me. And something you may not know, you also killed my wife. Upon hearing of Baldr's death, Frigg was filled with such grief that she tied a noose around her neck. What do you do with a man whom you've given everything to, and who repays you by murdering your son and wife, and turning your heir against you? You seek retribution. And so the question becomes, how do you seek retribution on a man you have sworn not to harm?"

Loki began to laugh. "What more can you do to me?"

"You think that you have nothing left, but I assure you, you still have much to lose." Odin waved his hand toward the servant. "Bring them in."

Loki's heart skipped a beat as he saw them. "Please don't do this." Sigyn and Nari walked toward the table. "Let them go," Loki pleaded.

Odin passed his hands through Nari's hair. "He's the spitting image of you, isn't he? Your son has grown up to be a fine man. You should be proud."

"Don't do this."

"For as long as the line of Farbauti lives, Jotunheim will always remain a threat to Asgard. Loki, you must understand that your father's line must end with you. For the greater good, of course."

Sigyn had once been beautiful. Her golden hair was now sprayed with grey, her bright blue eyes dull, and her smooth skin fell upon itself. "Odin, I beg you," she said, tears dripping down her cheeks. "Not my son, please, not my son." Nari didn't say a word, hiding his fear.

Odin produced the dagger. "Consider us even." He drove it through the boy's neck. Ribbons of red flowed out.

"I'm going to kill you," Loki said, gritting his teeth.

It was an unnatural laugh, originating from the foulest depths of depravity. Odin looked his brother in the eye and said, "We'll see about that."

CHAPTER THIRTY-FIVE

IT WAS a quiet night on the banks of the Iving, as was every night. Galvos had joined the watch three months prior. He had no false pretenses of what the job entailed: sleepless nights staring at a frozen-over lake. Rarely did anything ever come. If it did, it was usually a deer, and if it wasn't, it was a squirrel. His job was to stand, but if no one was looking, he allowed himself to sit. Boredom had dulled his senses to such an extent that when the arrow emerged from out of the darkness and landed by his feet, it took him a moment to even register it. He stood to attention the moment he did, noticing the small piece of paper attached to its tail. He yanked it off. "This is a warning. Stand down, allow us to pass, and you will be spared," the note read.

"Oi, if this is some kind of a joke, it's not funny," Galvos yelled into the unseen. Within seconds, another arrow landed by his feet. "Not a joke," the note attached to it said. Galvos ran. "Man your stations," he whaled.

It was a noise like thunder. The Aesir had placed three hundred of their finest soldiers on the banks of the Iving. Every last one of them shook as they heard the march. "I can't see," said one. "How many?" called another. Galvos strapped on his armor and stood by his brothers, side by side. "Hold the line," he said. "We are soldiers of Asgard.

Whatever comes our way, we will strike it down." Those were his last words. The spear tore through his skull, impaling the man standing behind him.

Six thousand Jotunns descended upon them. With spears and swords and arrows and axes and hammers, Fenrir and Jormungandr's army cut through the Aesir's border defenses like butter. The ice held, cracking but staying in place. Arrows, wreathed in flame, came crashing from the heavens. Few Jotunns fell, but those that did took ten Aesir with them. It was a cacophony of red and black, tinged with cries of mercy, and blades cutting them to silence.

"Three days," Fenrir roared as the crowd cheered. "Three days, and we will face Odin. What was done here was but a taste for the Aesir. They will know fear, they will know pain, and they will receive nothing but violence." He looked toward his brother. While everyone cheered and hollered, Jormungandr remained solemn. Fenrir walked toward him and kissed him on the cheek. "What troubles you? We've just had our first victory."

"That's precisely what troubles me," replied Jormungandr. "I need to speak to you in private." Fenrir nodded.

Although the bonfires could barely be seen, the army's celebrations made quiet speech difficult. "What's wrong?" Fenrir said. "They got twenty of us. We got three hundred of them. Odin doesn't stand a chance. In three days, our father will be free. What's got you worried?"

"Father," Jormungandr said. "What did you see in that fight?" Fenrir shrugged his shoulders. "Chaos, I saw chaos. In the heat of battle, instinct takes you. You kill and kill and kill, paying no mind to anything else. I have no doubt we'll win, but—" He stopped himself for a moment. "What if Father is killed in the fighting?"

Fenrir's smile faded. "What are you proposing? That we turn back?"

"No. By the gods, no. I need to get Father out of the way before the battle," Jormungandr said.

"And how are you going to do that?"

"Father spoke of a tunnel in the forest that allowed him and Thor to sneak in and out of the castle as boys. It's on father's map, the same map that got us this far. If I can find the tunnel, I can get into the castle and get Father out before the fighting begins."

Fenrir rubbed his lips and nodded. "Be careful. You go, you get Father, and you stay safe." He kissed Jormungandr on the forehead. "I'll see you on the battlefield."

CHAPTER THIRTY-SIX

Loki tightened his muscles, combatting the urge to shiver. Odin, surrounded by his personal guard, prodded him forward, out of the castle and into the field. Although she could've turned back, Sigyn followed. The ruckus of the army deadened as they moved farther away.

Odin raised his hand, stopping everyone in their tracks. He looked back at the vista. "It looks closer than it is," he said, motioning his head in the direction of the mountain in the distance. "From here, you would never know that it is a realm away. My father climbed Mount Surt every year, and every year, he'd make the summit faster than anyone I'd ever seen. It was there that he told me to take you as my brother. You were a child then. An innocent child locked in a dungeon, not unlike something from a fairy story. He'd had no idea the damage you'd sow. If he had anticipated this, he would've killed you himself. You see, my father was not averse to the murder of children. He never took any joy from it, but he was willing to make that call if it was for the greater good."

"Where are you taking me?" Loki said.

Odin grabbed one of the troop by the neck. "This man is one whom I trust." He rubbed the guard's hair. "His name is Hoenir, and he has served me well for six years. Do you know what I like the most about him? He's a decision-maker. Most people, when something needs to be done, come to me asking for permission. Not Hoenir. He knows what needs doing and does it." Odin motioned with his hand, and they began to walk once more. "Loki, my brother, do you remember Eitri? Of course you do—the greatest weapon-maker in the nine realms.

"You sought him out in your youth, sent word to Svartalfheim. Thor never had a weapon quite to his liking. Sometimes it was too heavy, sometimes too light. Unlike everyone else, he preferred hammers with shorter handles. You wanted to give him a gift for his name day and had Eitri fashion him something to his liking. Mjolnir, that's what he called it. And, as Thor often does, he ended up losing it within a month."

Odin pointed toward a small clay hut by the forest. "I had Eitri fashion me something too. Not a weapon in the traditional sense, but a tool for breaking men. I asked him to build something that would kill a man in the most painful way he knew how." He opened the door of the hut with the giddiness of a child opening a present. Loki's mouth dropped as he saw what was inside.

Dead snakes were tied to the support beams. The roof, which was domed from the outside and convex from the inside, was a large caul-dron. Green, acidic liquid dripped from a small tube in the ceiling. The metal restraints, attached to the wall, were below the dripping spigot.

"I leave you here, brother," Odin said. He turned to Hoenir. "Let the gods witness that I haven't told this man anything and, though I choose not to interfere, that I am innocent of anything he does."

Before Loki could react, Hoenir slammed him to the floor, drag-ging him toward the restraints. Sigyn wailed uncontrollably. Loki offered no resistance. He wasn't capable of any. Hoenir locked the restraints and stepped back.

Loki writhed as the liquid burned through his shirt, leaving dry scabs as it quickly evaporated. He bit his lip, trying his best not to give Odin the pleasure of hearing him scream. He clenched his muscles, holding in the wail as long as he could. Then, he relented. It came out of him, loud and terrible. Tears, uncontrollable and hot, followed.

"Murderer," Sigyn said under her breath. "Murderer." She jumped at one of the guards, pulling his shield from him. The guard looked to Odin, who, in turn, provided a nod of approval. Sigyn ran toward Loki, holding the shield as a bowl, cupping the acid.

Odin smiled and turned around, closing the door behind himself. "Come back for her in two days," he told Hoenir. "He'll be dead by then."

CHAPTER THIRTY-SEVEN

His FATHER HAD TOLD him of this place years ago, how he and Thor had played games in the seemingly unending blackness. Jormungandr's footsteps echoed through the dark, his father's words ringing in his ears. "Turn right three times, left, right again, walk fifty paces, climb, then walk straight." Leaves covered the door to the catacombs, leading him to believe that they hadn't been used in years. The smell was damp and thick, though not wretched. He dragged his fingers along the moist stone walls, feeling for the turns.

The rumbling came quietly at first, a gentle vibration. *Someone's here*, he thought, unsheathing his sword. It took him a moment to realize that the shaking wasn't coming from within the tunnels, or from the castle above, but from below the earth—a force gnawing at the surface, ready to plunge it into the abyss. He quickened his pace, hoping beyond hope that the structure wouldn't collapse on top of him. Then it stopped, replaced by the merciless calm.

A thin beam of light showed him the way. He thrust the door open only to find an Aesir soldier standing on the other side. They stared at each other blankly for a moment. Jormungandr smiled and thanked his lucky stars. He pulled the soldier into the catacombs, put his hand on the soldier's mouth, unsheathed his dagger, and plunged it below the Aesir's chin. An inaudible voice echoed in the back of his mind.

"Thank you," Jormungandr said as he stripped the soldier of his armor. "This is going to make things easier."

Years ago, Loki had told him that most soldiers stationed inside the castle, if not all of them, had just one job: to walk around aimlessly and pretend to be as imposing as possible. When he asked his father why, Loki replied, "Because those in high places only feel safe when they are surrounded by a bunch of idiots willing to die for them. Or at least do their bidding."

The armor was heavy. Worse than that, it was tight, especially around the shoulders and crotch, forcing him to walk with a hunched back. *How in the nine realms is someone supposed to fight wearing this?* he thought as he hobbled down the winding corridors.

"Soldier!" said the voice at the end of the corridor. "Back straight. Didn't I teach you better?"

"Apologies, sire," Jormungandr said, unable to see who he was speaking to through the small holes of the faceplate.

"Sire? Are you playing games, soldier? Address me in the proper fashion, or you will be flogged for insubordination."

"Sorry, sir. I didn't mean to offend."

"Sir?" gasped the Aesir. "Have you forgotten everything I taught you? Come here, let me take a good look at you."

Jormungandr shuffled forward, noticing the half-open door of what appeared to be an empty room. "What am I supposed to call you, oh great one?"

The Aesir's face grew red. "Come here, you son of a whore, so I can teach you some manners."

"Son of a whore? You're going to regret that." Jormungandr threw the cumbersome helmet to one side and, in one swift move, grabbed the Aesir by the shoulder, pushed him into the empty room, and slammed the door shut.

"Jotunn!" called the man.

Jormungandr dug the dagger between the plates of armor, into the

Aesir's side. "Speak, scream, call for help, make a single sound and I'll cut your dick off and feed it to you. Nod if you understand."

The Aesir nodded.

"I'm going to ask you some questions. If you answer them to the best of your ability, I might, maybe, possibly, let you walk out of here with all your limbs intact."

"I'm not telling you—"

Jormungandr twisted the blade. "I'm not done talking. Interrupt me again, and the sword goes in your asshole. Now, where were we? Ah, yes, if I so much as feel that you're lying to me, I'll twist. You lie to me again, I cut off a finger. Nod if you understand."

The Aesir did as he was asked.

"Where is he?"

The man's eyes shot open. "Who?"

Jormungandr twisted. "You know damn well who."

"Loki. You're looking for Loki."

Jormungandr smiled. "Right on the mark. Now, are you going to tell me where he is, or is that pinky coming off?"

"I don't know what it is that Odin had built. It's near the forest, just past the field. Looks like a hut from the outside. Odin had it built something special. Just for the Jotunn. That's all I know."

Jormungandr pulled out the dagger and pushed it toward the soldier's neck. The voice in the back of his mind grew louder, yet still inaudible.

"Please," said the soldier, "I have a daughter."

The blade shook in Jormungandr's hand. He could finally make out what the voice was saying. "Turn right three times, left, right again, walk fifty paces, climb, then walk straight." It belonged to his father. Then, another voice came—his own. "You don't want to do this. Not again. You don't want to do this." The soldier wept, his face a wet mess of regret. Jormungandr pulled the blade away and curled his fingers. He slammed his fist against the left side of the soldier's face, breaking his nose and knocking him out.

CHAPTER THIRTY-EIGHT

DRIP.

Clink.

The green liquid, a biting, venomous, vaporous acid, trickled from the spigot.

Drip.

Clink.

The shield grew heavy in Sigyn's arms.

Drip.

Clink.

It would be full soon, and when that happened it would dribble over her hands, cutting them, tearing through them, burning them with all of Odin's hate and malice. It would strike Loki in his heart, a pain far worse than any sword could bring.

Drip.

Clink.

She took a deep breath.

Drip.

Clink.

Steadied her hands.

Drip.

Clink.

And as fast as she could, she tipped the shield to one side, spilling its contents onto the floor. Smoke began to rise as the acid cut through stone. No, not smoke, a volatile vapor, horrible but quick to dissipate.

Drip.

Clink.

Loki screamed as the green venom collided with his chest. One drop. Two drops. Three. Each more terrible than the other, ripping through his shirt, searing flesh as it vanished into thin air. He shifted his body to the left then the right, looking for a way, any way, to escape from the inescapable.

Drip.

Clink.

Sigyn placed the shield over him. He breathed a sigh of momentary relief and looked up. "Why are you doing this?" She remained in place, silent, her gaze fixed on the spigot. "Tell me."

"He killed him, my son, the only one I lived for." Her voice was strong, stronger than Loki had ever heard it. "After you left, I didn't have anyone. Just him." *Hold it in*, she thought, resisting the luxury of tears. "I'm not letting him have this, have you. As far as I'm concerned, you're the only one I have left, and by the gods, I'm not letting him have you."

Loki wanted to protest, to tell her to leave, that she didn't owe him a thing, but he knew it wouldn't do anything. She'd made up her mind, delaying the inevitable. The green liquid, a biting, venomous, vaporous acid, trickled from the spigot.

Drip.

Clink.

CHAPTER THIRTY-NINE

THE CLIMATE WAS MORE temperate than it had been in months. The breeze swayed the forest's trees forwards and back. Admiring the weather, Heimdall stood atop the Tower, swinging his manhood in the air as if it were a windmill.

In the years since his adventure with Loki, Heimdall had taken on his responsibilities as Watcher with all the enthusiasm of an over-loaded mule. After all, he'd abandoned the Tower for the better part of six months, and no one was the wiser. Officially, he'd only left his post three times within that time period. In actuality, he'd spent more time away from the Tower than actually manning it.

Knowing of Odin's newfound willingness to invest in defense, his first official excursion was to ask for a horse. "A meager investment in our efforts to better protect the realm," Odin had said. His second official excursion was to pick up the horse, and his third excursion consisted of picking up another horse after the first horse grew ill and died (in truth, he'd lost it in a bet).

His want of a steed had little to do with being able to travel more quickly to the castle in the event that an enemy army was approach-ing. Rather, it was to help him travel the realm with greater speed and comfort.

Following his encounter with Baldr two decades prior, he'd chosen to remain in Fildred and wait for Loki for the better part of four months. When he finally returned to the Tower, he expected to find a party there ready to arrest him. Instead, he found six months' worth of food piled onto his doorstep, no questions asked. It was in that moment that he decided he would be better off returning to Fildred periodically, letting his demons fly loose for a few days, then going back to work doing nothing. Many of the townsfolk knew who he was, but as long as he kept visiting their taverns and brothels, they didn't care. Every time he left, he took with him enough wine to leave a bull catatonic.

Women and alcohol can fill a man for only so long. Inside, Heimdall felt a yearning for something more, something with meaning, with purpose. He had no idea what it would be or how he would go about getting it. But whenever that pang bloomed into consciousness, he swatted it away with grog and a large-breasted wench.

Nothing much, if anything at all, ran through his mind that day as he drunkenly stood swinging his cold, shriveled machismo. It took him more than a moment to realize there was no breeze. *Then how in the blazes are them trees moving?* He slapped himself in the face, hoping to knock the drunkenness out of himself. His eyes focused and his jaw dropped as he saw them marching through the trees. Jotunns. Thousands of them, an unending mass, shaking the world before them. He froze in place, every joint in his body trembling, and began to hyperventilate.

Then came a sound, unlike anything he'd heard before—roaring, loud, and terrible. Close yet far away. He fell to his knees as his eyes landed on the mountain in the distance. Surt. A realm away, but its power near. Just as Mimir had warned, the fire mountain had awoken. A cloud of grey and black bellowed from its top, painting the bright blue sky in darkness within mere minutes. A deep shaking pushed its way up the Tower. Rock and stone cracked beneath Heimdall's feet. He leaped up then sprinted down. The wooden support beams inside the tower shattered instantaneously into thousands of little pieces. Another shockwave followed, throwing him down the crumbling stairs. Impelled by a force he'd forgotten was inside of him, he rose as soon as he fell, wiping the blood dribbling down his forehead.

His shoulder smashed against the door, knocking it open. He rushed to the horse. It kicked, pushing him off as he attempted to mount it. He fell on his back, turning quickly as the horse's hooves came down near his head. Gasping, he grabbed the reins, brushing his fingers along the arch of the beast's nose. "It's alright, boy." Shards of yellow and orange jutted from the mountain. "I need you, and you need me. If we're going to get out of this, we're going to have to work together." The horse raised its two front feet and neighed loudly, finding its balance and planting itself. Heimdall pushed himself atop the creature's back and gave it a small kick.

He held the reins tight as it galloped. He looked back. The army was close enough to see him. Close enough to shoot him down. But the thick coverage of trees masked him from view. He breathed a sigh of relief. The world around him turned to a haze of vibration, green and brown, soon to be replaced by fire and death.

PART V
RAGNAROK

CHAPTER FORTY

JORMUNGANDR CLOSED HIS EYES, waiting for the tunnel to cave in around him. He pulled himself up, off the wet floor, his hands rubbing the cold damp of the walls. Beneath his fingers he could feel the earth slowly fracture, the steel-reinforced stone structure a trembling giant holding its ground. He took a deep breath. "Turn right three times, left, right again, walk fifty paces, climb, then walk straight." He darted, his legs propelling him faster than he realized. "Turn right three times, left, right again, walk fifty paces, climb, then walk straight."

Above him, the castle shook. Long-trapped dust flew in every direction, freed from every crack and crevice by the merciless vibration. Screams of panic cascaded through the castle's halls. Soldiers, taught to be fearless, cowered as they ran outside, greeted by a black and grey sky. Pillars cracked but did not collapse. Those outside stood transfixed, their eyes planted on the mountain in the distance. Fire, the likes of which no human mind can conjure, bellowed from its top —a harbinger of death, masked by the soon-to-be-gone canopy of nature. Amid the chaos, Asgard's king sat and waited for the storm to pass, not believing his end was nigh.

Thor rushed into the throne room. "We have to evacuate."

Odin took a sip of wine. "Nothing to worry about; it's too far."

"Are you mad?" Thor barked back. "Mimir was right. Surt is a fire mountain. We need to evacuate the castle, gather the troops, and evacuate Tilgrad and Pildur."

Odin chuckled. "What about the other towns? Are you going to leave them to burn?"

"Father, this is not a joke. The realm is doomed. We can at least save as many people as we can."

"Surt is a realm away. Do you think that the explosion will reach us?" Odin tapped the wooden chair. "My family, our family, has ruled these lands for over a hundred generations. I don't believe our ruin will come at the hands of a mountain."

"Your rule is at an end, Father, whether you care to believe it or not. Stay here if you want to. I'm going to save our people." Thor walked toward the door.

"If you order the evacuation of this castle, I will have you imprisoned for treason," Odin said behind him.

Thor stopped. Inside of him, a feeling he'd known had always been there, but pushed deep down, came rushing to the surface of his mind: pure, unadulterated hate. "You've doomed us." The words came out gently. He slammed the door shut behind him and marched out into the black of noon.

Jormungandr crashed into the wooden door, breaking it from its hinges. In the distance, he saw it—the red and yellow glow permeating the horizon, chasing the dark clouds. He shook in terror. Every bone in his body compelled him to run, to abandon his mission, to run back to the army and warn them. But he couldn't. Not now. There it was—the small hut by the forest.

Father.

The faint silhouette of a rider bloomed from out of the black, rushing toward the hut. Jormungandr produced his bow, took aim, and fired. The rider swerved, dodging the shot, and all the others that followed it. Jormungandr unsheathed his sword and planted himself in front of the cabin. The rider continued to rush forward. The moment he'd reached striking distance, Jormungandr swung. Startled, the horse raised its two front feet, threw the rider to the ground, and ran off into the distance.

Thor grunted as he got up. "You don't want to do this, son."

Jormungandr leaped forward. Thor raised his shield, blocking the strike.

Sigyn's arms grew weak. She tried everything she could to ignore the noise outside. The green liquid had corroded the lining on the inside of the shield. Loki looked up and smiled. In his mind, he planned his words, searching for the combination that might compel her to leave him. But there was no time for that. He could hear the fighting outside. "Can you hear that?" he asked.

She nodded.

"You need to get out of here."

"I'm not leaving you."

"How long do you think you can keep holding that thing? Can't you see it? I'm already dead. You're just prolonging the inevitable. Please, I'm begging you, leave me. Get away from here. Find a life far away and never turn back toward this miserable place."

She shot him a look he'd never seen before—not one of anger, but of curiosity. "It's burning away the inside of the shield." She motioned her head at the green liquid dripping from the spigot. "You think if I pour some of it onto your restraints, you'll be able to break free?"

He took a deep breath. Had he been able to shrug his shoulders, he would have. "Worth a shot. Do your worst, woman."

Thor stayed defensive as Jormungandr attacked, waiting for him to tire. Jormungandr hacked away at the shield, cutting through the metal binding. Thor fell to his knees. He rolled out of the way as his opponent's blade came down and hit the grass. He regained his footing, hitting Jormungandr square in the chest with his hammer. Jormungandr stiffened his body, stopping himself from falling over. Before he knew it, another hammer strike came. A crunching sound burst out from his ribs. He coughed blood, spat, and dodged the third blow. He raised his sword, bringing it down upon Thor's shoulder. Not having pierced through the armor, the sword was stuck. Thor head-butted him, stepped back, and struck at his feet. Jormungandr grabbed the back of Thor's head. They toppled together.

Thor placed his knees atop Jormungandr's hands. His fists came down like thunder. Jormungandr began to swallow blood. His teeth danced free in his mouth. A bolt of energy burst through him, giving him just enough strength to break one hand free. With it, he reached for his side and pulled out the dagger. Pain exploded in every cell of his body. Ignoring it, he raised his fist, digging the blade into the side of Thor's neck. He pulled the knife out, and dug it in again, and again, and again.

Thor tried to scream. Nothing came out but a garbled mess.

Loki bit down on his lip. The liquid made a hissing sound as it hit his chest. Sigyn took careful aim, positioning the shield toward the metal restraints. "Quickly, woman," Loki barked, his eyes watering. Just as she was about to pour, the door swung open. She dropped the shield. The green acid landed within an inch of Loki's head. Before a word could be said, Jormungandr grabbed her by the neck, his face half-covered in blood. He raised the dagger.

"No, wait!" Loki yelled.

Jormungandr threw her to one side and, without missing a beat, dug his sword into the small gap between the metal plate holding the cuffs into the wall. The bolts broke from their position, taking bits of stone with them as they dropped to the floor. Loki rubbed his wrists, not yet able to realize what had just happened. Jormungandr pulled him to his feet.

"My boy." Tears flowed freely from Loki's eyes as he hugged his son. "I thought you were—"

"We're fine, both of us, me and Fenrir."

"You're hurt."

"I can manage," Jormungandr lied through the fleshy mess where his front teeth used to be. "We need to get you out of here as soon as possible and warn the army."

"Army?"

"Fenrir and I might've let it slip that you're the rightful king of Jotunheim. That managed to reunite the realm. We have an army six thousand strong not too far from here, ready to root Odin out." He waited for his father to scold him.

"Good," Loki said. "I told that bastard I was going to kill him, and I intend on keeping that promise." He paused for a moment, gathering his thoughts. "Magni and Modi?"

"They're with us. They're safe." Jormungandr wiped the dripping red out of his eyes. "We need to tell the army to retreat."

Loki shot his son a searching look.

"Whatever revenge you had planned for Odin, it seems like the mountain is going to take care of it for you." He stepped back, allowing his father to see the dark outside through the open door. "It's not nighttime. Surt—that's the name of the mountain, right? I thought they only existed in fairy stories, but it turns out they're real. Surt is a fire mountain."

Loki rubbed his chin. "Ragnarok," he said under his breath. "Mimir's warning." He closed his eyes, in his mind painting a map of Asgard. "The army's not retreating. Tilgrad and Pildur . . . if you took the pass by the Iving, you must have passed by them?"

"We did."

"Thousands of innocent men, women, and children live in those towns. Knowing Odin, he's too damn stubborn and proud to evacuate his people. We have to do it. Take them with us back to Jotunheim."

As they walked outside, Loki heard a muffled voice, trying to speak but unable to. His eyes landed on Thor lying on his back, his hand pressed to the side of his neck in a feeble attempt to contain the bleeding. "No, no, no, no," Loki gasped as he ran to Thor's side. He placed Thor's head atop his knee and rubbed his hair. Thor wheezed, his words a blood-coated and incomprehensible muddle of meaninglessness. "Your sons, they're safe. I promise you. I'll watch over them, protect them, just as you protected me." Thor outstretched his free hand. Loki held it tightly. A faint hint of a smile formed on the edges of Thor's lips as he breathed his last.

Jormungandr could feel it, blood sloshing about inside of him, going into places it shouldn't. It was slow, dripping into his lungs. Feigning strength, he walked to his father. "I am so sorry. I had no idea who he was."

Loki nodded, wiping his eyes. "He came here to free me."

Jormungandr gripped his chest. "I'm so sorry, Father." He dropped to his knees, his eyes red, his limbs trembling. Loki turned to meet his gaze. He slumped over to one side, his breath quickening before ceasing.

CHAPTER FORTY-ONE

THE TENTS and wooden huts which housed the troops surrounding the castle lay in pieces. Men clamored toward the gate, pushing one another, hoping that when it opened—if it opened—they would be allowed inside. Cracks decorated the towering stone walls. *It had to be the shaking,* Heimdall thought. His eyes darted upwards, towards the archers. *Can they hear me?* "I am the Watcher," he yelled with as much strength as his lungs could muster. "I am the Watcher." The troops continued to push, not knowing it was even more dangerous to be inside. The flame bursting from the tip of the mountain licked the sky. "I have to see Odin," he pleaded to anyone who would listen. "We are under attack. I am the Watcher. An army comes from the north. From Jotunheim."

The archers stared at him. "He's lying. He wants to get inside," one of them said.

"What if he's telling the truth?" said another.

"We can't bloody well open the gate. It'll be anarchy."

Heimdall pushed through the crowd of four thousand men, trained to kill and die, begging to live. The archers drew their arrows, aimed, and dropped the rope. The troops rushed toward it. Arrows

179

flew at whoever attempted the climb. "Only him," roared one of the archers, pointing at Heimdall. "Only the Watcher. Anyone else tries to climb, and we won't hesitate to fire."

He could hear them. Cries for help, wails of "let us in" and "please don't shoot." As he reached the top, a barrage of hands grabbed him and pulled.

"Where's Odin?" Heimdall said, gasping for air.

"Inside," said an archer.

Without pause or hesitation, Heimdall rushed inside. He kept his eyes forward, doing his best to ignore the howling and wailing. Soldiers guarded the entrances, stopping anyone who might attempt to leave. Cries of women and children echoed through the winding passageways. He ran past the two guards stationed in front of the throne room and pushed the door open. "We're under attack. Jotunns. Thousands of them, marching from the north."

Odin's eyes widened. "Are you sure of what you saw?"

"They're crossing the forest as we speak."

"How many?"

"Thousands. Maybe five or six thousand. We're outnumbered."

"Loki," Odin muttered under his breath. He looked to one of the men by the door. "Bring me Hoenir."

———

As they walked down the corridor, Hoenir listened intently to his king's words.

Odin looked outside toward the men stationed on the wall. "Our archers are in position, but our infantry is in complete disarray. We need them in position. If they're not ready, if they're disorganized and disoriented, the Jotunns will carve through them like butter."

"Sire, the men are terrified," Hoenir replied.

"Then, they will find their courage when they see their king fighting beside them."

"Sire, all due respect, but do you think—"

"Boy, if you're about to say what I think you're about to say, you'd better not. I fought the Jotunns on the hills of Geirrod before your mother sucked a tit. Find Thor and order our troops to man their positions. Tell them I will be fighting with them, side by side."

There was an eerie silence as the gate opened. Armor was heavier than Odin remembered. He hadn't worn it in over four decades. They looked at him with reverence as he walked forward. To his left were legionnaires, armed with pikes and spears. Atop the wall, archers scanned the vista; their eyes fixed on the Jotunn hordes emerging from the forest. The infantry stationed in front did not carry with them the round shields of their comrades. Instead, their shields were tall, taller than any man. In their left hand were spears, sharp and long. Riders on horseback shaped the middle position of the formation.

Odin stood at the front. "There is our enemy. They come here to kill every soul in Asgard. As we stand here today, the mountains themselves call to the heavens, praying for our victory. The fate of this blessed realm lies in your hands. Jotunheim has risen. A Jotunn knows only violence. Only blood. We will repay violence with violence, blood with blood. We will chase them back across the Iving. Whatever they throw at you, throw it right back. Whatever they give you, return it twofold. Soldiers of Asgard, this is what you've spent your lives training for."

"For Asgard!" called a distant voice. The call was reciprocated and repeated. Through their fear, through the urge to run, they chanted. Men hit their shields with their swords. The sound, which was not unlike thunderous applause, boomed through the air into the distance.

Unlike the others, Hoenir was calm, his eyes fixed on the enemy and his heart heavy with bad news. "Have you found Thor?" Odin said to him. "Have you found my son?"

"He was last sighted riding out of the castle."

Odin's mind began to drift, conjuring the endless possibilities, the scenarios which ended with Thor captured or worse. "Ride out with me," he told Hoenir. "Call on Heimdall. A loyal servant is a rarity. He rides with us. I have fought Jotunns multiple times before. An unruly lot, but they do possess honor. I wish to speak with their leader, whoever that may be. If my son is with them, I have to know."

CHAPTER FORTY-TWO

THE WORLD COULDN'T END. Not now. Not again. Too much was at stake. Ragnarok had come.

Loki stared at his shaking hand, trying to steady it. He was on his knees. His eyes were dripping rubies. *They can't see me like this*, he thought as the endless horde of Jotunn soldiers emerged from behind the tree line. The gap between the forest and the castle was just over two miles. This army had walked hundreds of miles, he knew, but if they walked two more, it would mean their complete and total annihilation. Their footsteps, seemingly infinite, beat the cold earth like drums. Loki focused on the man walking at the front. Though he could not see his face, he'd known his presence, the way he walked, held himself when he wanted to project a sort of strength he didn't quite believe he possessed. His son, Fenrir. Loki lowered his gaze once more, fixing it upon the two bodies which, up until recently, had belonged to Thor and Jormungandr. His son and the closest thing he'd had to a brother, and he couldn't mourn them. *No time for that.* Sigyn stood in silence, not knowing what to do or what to say or if there was, in fact, anything to be said or done.

"This has to mean something," Loki said. The words came out of him but originated not from within, but from a place far away, spilling out of him an old, hard message. "All of this. It has to be for something." He placed his hand on his son's head and began to stroke his hair. "This has to mean something," he said once more. He raised his hand again. It was shaking even more furiously now. He curled his fingers into a fist and pushed himself off the ground. He looked to Sigyn. "This is it. The 'why.' The 'why' of it all. All this pain. All this misery. This, right now, is the 'why.'"

She looked at him, puzzled at what she was hearing. No, not puzzled; people have said far stranger things when facing death. Rather, she was mystified. Unable to grasp any meaning from what had just occurred, or indeed, what was now happening. Loki hoisted Jormungandr over his shoulder and placed his body by the hut. He put Thor's body next to his son's. He placed a kiss on both their foreheads. "I'll see you soon," he said. He didn't think that he could bring himself to do it, but in times of sheer necessity, people often do what they previously thought they couldn't. He removed Jormungandr's silver Aesir armor, leaving the black shirt underneath. Loki equipped himself with his son's armor, sword, and bow, as well as Thor's hammer.

The horse neighed in the distance, running in aimless circles. Loki clicked his tongue, calling to it. It turned and, as if summoned by a force not of this world, walked to him. Loki rubbed its nose and gripped the reins. "Ride," he said to Sigyn, holding the reins out to her. "Get as far away from here as you can."

She shook her head. "You take it." She could see right through him. His feigned strength and conviction. He was terrified, a bruising fright that would've taken a great many other men. "You need it." She smiled. "I can't ride anyway. Don't know how," she lied.

"Run. Run as fast as your legs can carry you. Cross the Iving." He paused for a moment, knowing that in all probability, the next words to come out of his mouth would be a complete and utter lie. "When this is all over, I'll find you." She hugged him, kissed him on the cheek, and disappeared into the dark of the forest.

There was a large *clack* sound as fifty Jotunn archers withdrew their arrows from their quivers. "Hold," Fenrir said, raising his arm into the air, his eyes fixed on the lone figure riding from the east. The fire mountain roared in the distance, spluttering molten rock thousands of feet into the air. Fenrir ignored it but knew the fear it incited in his men. The rider drew closer. Fenrir could hear the bowstrings tighten. "Hold." His jaw dropped as he began to make out the details of the approaching shadow. "Lower your bows," he commanded. "Lower your bows!"

Though two miles away, Fenrir could hear the Aesir army's ruckus as if it were right beside him. He furrowed his brow, placing all his focus on the lone rider. "Could it be?" he whispered to himself and then smiled. "Long live the king!" he roared. "Long live Loki of Jotunheim!" The horde erupted into yells and cries of jubilation; such was their sound that the clashing of the Aesir's shields grew inaudible.

As he drew closer, Loki pulled back the reins, unsheathed his son's sword, and pointed it toward the heavens. He provided the steed with a gentle kick. It bolted, galloping toward the Jotunn army. A part of Loki couldn't believe it. How could these men, men he'd never sat with, never talked to, be willing to travel such distances and give their lives for him? A part of him wanted to laugh at the ludicrousness of it all. He held himself, not allowing himself to do anything of the sort. In rapid succession, the army fell to its knees and within an instant was silent.

"Long live Loki Laufeyson, son of Farbauti, king of Jotunheim," Fenrir said, his head pointed toward the ground. To his right was an older man, and to his left, Loki recognized, were Magni and Modi.

Loki unmounted the steed and walked toward them. "Rise." As soon as the final syllable left his lips, six thousand men rose to their feet. Once again, the urge came back to Loki, compelling him to laugh, to tell them they were fools for traveling so far to save a man they had no business saving. "This has to mean something," he whispered to himself. He took a deep breath and puffed out his chest. "Men of Jotunheim." Spearmen smacked the butts of their weapons on the ground. Swordsmen struck their shields with their blades, a demonstration that they hung on to every word he spoke. He pulled Fenrir in close. "We have to pull the army back. If they attack, we're all dead," he whispered into his son's ear. Fenrir's face contorted, but just as he was about to protest, Loki shot him a look Fenrir could not remember ever seeing on his father's face. Loki's eyes drifted to Magni and Modi. "Do they know?" he asked his son. Fenrir nodded. "Good. It'll make this easier."

He pulled his shoulders back and took another deep breath. He stepped forward. "Men of Jotunheim, this is your hour. Fate has chosen you. You come to this land as conquerors. I ask you to leave it as heroes." The crowd began to howl. As soon as it did, Loki placed his index finger to his lips, and there was silence once more. "Ragnarok is upon us. A foretold fire of endless destruction." Loki pulled out his sword and pointed it toward the mountain. From the corner of his eye, he could see three figures riding toward them from the Aesir army. He paid them no mind and turned back to face his men. "Surt burns and its flames will envelop this realm, killing all in it." The crowd cheered in pure ecstasy. Loki raised his arm into the air. "What brave men you are, cheering for the death of innocents." All sound faded.

Loki began to pace back and forth. "You there," he said to the first man his eyes landed upon, "who is your enemy?"

The man stepped forward. "Asgard," he said nervously.

"Be gone," Loki barked back. "I have no use for you." Fenrir's jaw dropped. All around voices began to emanate—whispers, talk, an intense yet quiet discomfort, like an itch at the back of one's throat. Loki walked toward the man. He grabbed him by the breastplate and pulled him close. "Tell me, was it the farmers or tradesmen that ordered Jotunheim's borders be sealed? Perhaps it was the fishermen or tailors who ordered our land be invaded, our cities, towns, and villages burned, our women dishonored, our children slaughtered, and our very way of life be brought to ruin?"

The man took a gulp. "No," he whispered, his voice a husk of its former self.

"Over twenty years ago, a man nearly gave his life defending

Jotunheim," Loki said. "Today, he sacrificed his life to save mine. His sons stand amongst you. The man I speak of is Thor Odinson. What imaginary boundaries we place, whatever we call ourselves, Jotunn or Aesir, he saw beyond it. To him, there was one universal truth. Human life is sacred—something to be preserved. I owe my life to him. As do all of you."

The man raised his head and walked forward. Six thousand pairs of eyes lay upon him, waiting, watching. "What would you have me do, my king?" the man said, his voice now loud, finding what it was that it had lost.

"Destiny has granted us our retribution," Loki said. "But it has also cast upon us, all of us, a responsibility. The heir to Asgard's throne gave his life to a people that were not his own. It is now our job to do the same." Asgard's geography appeared before Loki's eyes. "The towns of Tilgrad and Pildur, you passed them on your way here, did you not?" He looked into the distance. The three riders drew closer. "Odin," he said under his breath, hoping that no one had heard him. Louder, he said, "We must evacuate them. More than twenty thousand lives are at stake."

The old man standing beside Fenrir coughed a feigned cough, one that would draw attention. "Sire," Lyfinder said, "I'm also afraid to ask, but . . . is that our enemy?" He pointed toward the three approaching figures.

Loki nodded, and as soon as he did, every archer within earshot drew an arrow and aimed their bow. "Say the word, sire, and he's done for."

"Keep your weapons on him, but hold your fire. Odin's a tricky one. Never know when he's got something up his sleeve. If he alerts your suspicions, shoot to kill," Loki said. "You, you, you, and you." Loki pointed at Fenrir, Magni, Modi, and Lyfinder. "Ride out with me."

CHAPTER FORTY-THREE

A BROAD SMILE spread across Odin's lips. He began to clap as Loki approached. "My, my, I'd always known you were one step ahead, but this—" He motioned with his arms at the seemingly infinite army stationed by the tree line. "—is impressive. I must admit I've underestimated you. Managing to rally a realm to your cause, in secret, well, that might be the greatest trick you've ever pulled off." His expression changed, darkening. "Where's Thor?"

"Odin, son of Borr, I have come here to discuss terms," Loki said.

"Terms of your surrender?" Odin smiled again. "Very wise. Mimir taught you well."

Loki hid whatever hatred and annoyance he felt, masking the emotions in a facade of determination. "We do not seek war, Odin. Mimir was right. Ragnarok has come. More than twenty thousand innocent men, women, and children live in the towns of Tilgrad and Pildur. We ask that your men lay down their arms and help us evacuate their countrymen."

"Ragnarok," Odin laughed. "Mimir was right. So what? Surt's too far away to be a threat."

"Are you blind?" Loki barked back. The mountain was now wreathed in flame, spitting balls of fire into the air. "If you aren't going to save your people, order your men to stand down and don't get in our way."

Odin's shoulder shook as he fell into laughter. "Your army turns, and we will chase them. We will cut them down one by one until there is nothing left but you. And as for you, my brother, you'll go back into that hole." He motioned his head toward the hut. "However, if you hand me back my son, I'll let you do as you wish. Take Tilgrad and Pildur. What do I care?"

Loki's lips began to tremble. Words rushed through his head, but before he could say anything, Modi stepped forward. "Grandfather," he said, "my father is fallen. He died freeing my king."

"Grandfather?" Odin mumbled. "Thor's sons? Thor is dead?" Although Loki had seen madness in Odin's eyes before, this was something different. An unbreakable rage, the demon gaze of a tortured soul. "You are no grandson of mine. A Jotunn bastard. Nothing more."

"I am Asgard's rightful heir, whether you like it or not. You will lead this land to ruin because you are too scared to let go of power," Modi said.

"It doesn't have to be this way," Loki said. "Odin, it's not too late. Help me save your people." He paused for a moment. "*Our* people, and everything will be forgiven. I will seek no retribution. You will live as a free man. You can know your grandchildren."

"You've taken everything from me," Odin said. "If the realm burns, it burns. But not before I see to it that everything you love burns too."

Heimdall looked down and gave his horse a small kick. It began to canter forward. He pulled the reins, instructing it to turn, bringing himself shoulder to shoulder with Loki.

"What are you doing?" hissed Odin.

"I intend to fight for Asgard," Heimdall replied. "If it means that I have to fight you, then so be it."

Odin looked back toward his home. Just as he was about to go, he stopped himself. "I should've killed you. As my father dropped to his knees, crying like a child, I should have plucked you out of his hands and slit your throat." He regained his composure. "Whatever should happen to you on the battlefield, let the gods bear witness that my men only acted in self-defense and not by my order." He gave his horse a small kick and was off, Hoenir at his back.

"That could've been worse," Lyfinder said. "Nothing to worry about, sire. A Jotunn is worth ten Aesir on the battlefield."

"I hope that you're not exaggerating," Loki said. "What comes next might depend on it."

"Five hundred men against four thousand," Lyfinder gasped. "That's suicide."

They were close to the army, but out of earshot. Loki had slowed down his steed's pace to that of a snail, hoping to buy himself a few more precious moments. The others followed suit. "If we fall back as we are, Odin's troops will be able to close in on us. Rather than mounting an evacuation, we'd be fighting a battle. We need a contingent to stay behind and fight."

"Stay behind and die, you mean," Fenrir said.

"No," Loki said. "The castle has a weakness. An unprotected penetration point."

"The catacombs," Heimdall supplied.

"Exactly," Loki replied. "Five hundred men will stage an offensive, striking head-on with everything they've got. How many archers on the wall?"

"Three hundred," Heimdall said.

"Then we'll need thirty men to infiltrate the castle through the catacombs and take on the archers from behind."

"Then we'll have the high ground," Fenrir said.

"Exactly," Loki replied. "Once we've taken the wall, it'll be like catching fish in a barrel."

"This just might work," Heimdall said.

"I like your confidence," Loki said, "because you're going to lead them through the tunnels."

Heimdall nodded. "We're going to need a way to get our men on the field up onto the wall, to safety. More men, more arrows. We can finish this quickly."

"And how are we going to do that?" Fenrir said.

"Rope," Heimdall said. "Plenty of it at the Tower."

"And the evacuation?" Lyfinder inserted.

"You, Fenrir, Magni, and Modi will lead it. Split the army in two. One half goes to Pildur and the other to Tilgrad."

"That's not going to happen," Fenrir said. "I'm not leaving your side. Not again."

"This isn't an open discussion. You're helping with the evacuation and staying the hell away from the battlefield."

"Like hell I am," Fenrir snarled. "Where you go, I go."

Loki wanted to protest, but he'd seen this look in Fenrir's eyes before and knew there was no point in arguing the matter. Instead, he turned to Lyfinder. "Gather the men. Get them into position as fast as you can."

CHAPTER FORTY-FOUR

TICK.

Tick.

Tick.

Tick.

Tick.

It was a sound not unlike that of rain falling on sheets of steel. But it was not rain. It was the vibration. A slight tremor echoing from the depths of the earth. A warning call.

Odin felt it growing beneath his feet, and for the very first time he entertained the possibility that Mimir might've been right. A part of himself, he suspected, always believed, always knew. But to know was to leave, to let go of everything, to drag the names of his ancestors through the dirt by relinquishing his crown and moving his people to foreign lands, forever leaving them as second-class citizens. He glanced upwards and, at that moment, found relief.

The endless horde of Jotunns began to disappear back into the trees. In a head-to-head fight, he couldn't beat them. He knew it. But, running with their backs turned, the Jotunns would prove easy targets. He called for his men to advance. The sound that was unlike that of rain falling on sheets of steel was replaced by a deep, pulsing hum as the four-thousand-strong army began to march in formation.

Within moments, every single last Jotunn had disappeared from view. It might've been a fifteen-minute walk, but it felt like an eternity. Odin unsheathed his sword, pointing it at the forest. But just as he was about to tell his men to attack, to find every single last Jotunn and cut them down, arrows, hundreds of them, came flying from behind the tree line. The Aesir scampered to bring their shields up, but the projectiles came with such speed and such consistency the Aesir fell by their hundreds. Amid the barrage, Odin would've been shot, would've fallen before he could utter a single word, had Hoenir not covered him with his shield.

It was not a noise most live to hear—the sound of death herself, a sweet yet terrible utterance of war. The far cries of the Jotunns grew deeper, taking shape, solidifying and blooming as they broke past the tree line. Odin pushed the shield off of himself and stood. "To your king," Hoenir yelled. Disorganized Aesir troops rushed around their monarch.

They raised their shields, blocking the barrage of arrows, which did not come from above, but from the front. Odin looked up to see the Jotunn charging. Not a Jotunn, but *the* Jotunn. Loki's arrows landed with precision, finding the gaps between the plates of armor. "Kill him!" Odin wanted to yell. "Shoot him down. Cut him down. Kill him!" Instead, he bit his tongue. A wave of hands grabbed hold of him, pulling him back, away from the projectiles.

Hoenir roared as he charged, lunging at Loki, swinging his broadsword. Loki swerved to the left and withdrew two arrows from his quiver. The first bounced off of Hoenir's breastplate, but the second managed to squeeze its way into the gap at the side of the Aesir's armor. Hoenir pulled it out, threw it aside, and charged ahead.

Like ants pouring out of a hole that had just been filled with poison, what remained of the Jotunn army came gushing out of the forest. Had the Aesir been organized, with a well-positioned front line, they might've been able to impede the charge. But the Aesir, out of position and in disarray, found themselves overwhelmed by swords and spears from the anterior and arrows raining down from atop.

Hoenir swung the sword with fury and speed; at first his moves were measured, precise, but as his foe dodged each and every blow, keeping himself out of striking range, Hoenir began to swing madly in every direction, hoping the wild blade would meet its target.

Loki swerved left then right, rolling backward, jumping back onto his feet as fast as he'd landed on the ground. He kept a tight grip on the three arrows, two of them to be a distraction and one of them to maim. Hoenir's armor was thicker than that of his comrades, more padded. Nothing could kill him but a close strike. Loki knew that. But getting too close to the towering giant, Loki also knew, would mean a swift and gruesome death.

Hoenir lunged once more. Loki darted to the right, firing the first of the three arrows at his enemy's head. Hoenir raised his arms. The arrow broke on the metal plate covering his forearm. Loki took the opportunity, firing the second in the same direction as the first and the third right into the gap underneath Hoenir's armpit. Hoenir screamed, and for one singular moment, the world around him disappeared, replaced by nothing but red. It was a moment, but a moment was all that Loki needed. He sprinted forward, pulled out Thor's hammer, and brought it down with all his strength atop Hoenir's head. The helmet crumpled, producing a sharp *crack*. A spray of red shot from the helmet's eye holes as the body landed lifelessly on the grass.

"Back!" Odin screamed, batting away the hands that were dragging him. "Back to the wall." His wailing vanished into the chaos, the needless chirping of a bird informing the lion of where the antelope lay. Running with what strength remained to carry them, the Aesir rushed toward the castle. But no matter how far or how fast they ran, they found no reprieve from the hell raining down from above or the swords and spears below.

Boom!

A large cloud of red, yellow, and black burst from the mountain, shooting balls of fire and molten stone thousands of feet into the air.

Although every urge in his body commanded him to turn back, Loki marched on. "Forward," he yelled, his sword smeared in red. His men, none of whom knew him, all of whom were ready to die for him, followed. "For Jotunheim!"

The mountain's missiles crashed into the castle. Odin turned, his face paler than it had been when his father passed. The base of the spire that had once housed the counsel's chamber shattered into a thousand little pieces. The tower, as if it hadn't comprehended what had just happened, stood firm for the blink of an eye, then hurtled down. The spire landed atop the wall. Brick and shards of glass flew every which way. Odin stood, shaking, tears flowing down his cheeks. "What have I done?" he muttered to himself. All sound vanished. A calm yet infuriating *hiss* pervaded his hearing. He looked up to the men on the wall. "Fire, damn it!"

A thousand arrows covered the sky, a reflection of what was coming. "Shields!" screamed Loki at the top of his lungs. There was a thunderous *thrunk* as the Jotunn infantrymen pushed their shields out toward the heavens.

Tick.

Tick.

Tick.

Tick.

Tick.

The arrows landed upon them but did not impede them. "Reform the line," Loki said. From all around, his men circled him, moving in a manner that might lead one to believe that they'd spent their entire lives training for this moment. Spearmen stood at the front, swordsmen behind, and archers at the very back. They waited as the arrows landed. *Tick. Tick. Tick. Tick. Tick.* Waiting for the right moment. *Tick. Tick. Tick. Tick. Tick.* "Attack!" Loki roared, seeing the clearing. The line broke and cut straight into the Aesir's formation. The archers on the wall lowered their bows, knowing that if they were to shoot, they would kill their own countrymen.

Through the chaos, Odin's eyes met Loki's. Loki removed four arrows from his quiver. Odin's pulse quickened. *Thump. Thump.*

Thump. Loki took careful aim, letting two fly simultaneously. They struck the two guards standing by the Aesir king. *Thump. Thump. Thump.* Loki closed an eye. *This is it,* he thought. But before he could fire, a ball of molten rock from the heavens landed not twenty feet in front of him, throwing him on his back. He coughed and looked up. *I can't hear. I can't hear. I can't hear!* He began to hyperventilate.

Odin turned to the men atop the wall. "Shoot!"

"If we fire, we'll be killing our own men!" one of the archers said.

"Shoot!"

As soon as the command was given, the arrows came, killing three Aesir for every Jotunn.

CHAPTER FORTY-FIVE

ALTHOUGH THE OUTSIDE structure stood firm and seemingly undamaged, the stairs that wound up the inside of the Tower of Sight had collapsed, burying with them the entrance to the basement. Heimdall heaved as he pulled the crushed rock bricks that stood in his way, praying silently that he wouldn't be buried the next time the earth shook. He flung open the door to see that the wooden steps had also succumbed to the shaking. He patted the soldier's back. "After I get it, I'm going to throw the rope up. You dangle it down and pull me out." The soldier nodded.

Heimdall jumped down, braced himself, and landed on his back. He moaned and grunted as he stood up, then smiled as he realized that the contents of the basement, which were piled up on top of each other to such an extent that very little had moved, or could move for that matter, remained precisely as he'd left them.

He had no idea which of the Tower's previous caretakers had had a penchant for climbing, but Heimdall was glad he did. Dust had collected atop the wooden crate, only half of it from the tremors. Heimdall opened it and checked the integrity of its contents. After taking a moment to test the rope's sturdiness, he began to search for a lightweight bag. He found a bag most suited to his need hidden under a pile of old books that no one had ever bothered to read. "I'm about to throw it up," he said as he walked back to where the stairs had been.

———

Staring into the dark chasm, Fenrir struggled to keep his balance as the tremor came. His eyes darted to the clearing above the forest. While the mountain was hidden, Fenrir could see the fire spitting from its top. He shook his head, hoping to shake out the dark images clouding his thoughts, and stared back down at the entrance to the dark and seemingly endless tunnel. He recalled how his father had spoken of this place, of how he and Thor would play games in the dark, and found it hard to believe that such a place had ever been an abode of joy.

"Took your sweet time," he said, hearing the crunch of dry leaves under the Aesir's footsteps.

Heimdall ignored the comment and pulled out a long, thick rope from the bag on his back. The men circled him. "It's easy to get lost in there. You won't be able to see anything, and anything you can hear won't be able to hear you. You don't want to get lost in there, or worse, end up in the wrong part of the castle. The catacombs go through the castle like veins through a body." He held out the rope. "Everyone grab hold, and no matter what happens, don't let go."

One of the soldiers coughed. "It won't collapse on top of us, will it?" he said nervously.

"It might," Heimdall said. "But if it does, it means that the whole castle's come down. You might not be able to see it, but the walls are reinforced with steel. Any more questions?" The men remained silent. Heimdall turned to Fenrir. "They got any good brothels in Jotunheim? Because that's the first place I'm going when all this shit's over."

Fenrir laughed. "If there aren't any, we'll open one." He paused for a moment. "*If* we get out of this."

The tunnels seemed to stretch into eternity. Heimdall, who was walking at the front of the line, had tied the rope around his waist, freeing his hands to feel for the turns. He was worried that the stairs would prove difficult but was pleased to see that the inverse was true. "Not much longer," he said, recognizing the lone, thin line of light. They came toppling, one on top of the other, as they rushed out of the door. Fenrir gripped his sword tightly, sure that someone had heard them. He looked up at the red room they'd emerged into. Although it was a place he'd never seen before, there was something familiar about it. "Quiet," he hissed back at his comrades.

"Don't worry," Heimdall said. "No one's been in here for years. Sigyn abandoned it long ago. Too many memories, she said." Fenrir shot him a curious look, spurring Heimdall to elaborate. "This was, long ago, your father's living quarters."

"Where to now?" Fenrir said, not allowing himself to take the place in, to think of what sort of life his father had once lived here.

"The balconies give us the best vantage point," Heimdall said, stuffing the rope back into the bag. "It's a good vantage point. We'd be higher than the archers on the wall. We'll be able to shoot them. They won't be able to shoot us."

Heimdall had expected to find the castle in chaos, but as they walked down the winding corridors, toward the northern wing balconies, he didn't see a soul. Official procedure in the event of an attack on the castle, he knew, was that all non-combatants (primarily servants) were to gather in the dining hall on the ground floor. "They're all going to die." He caught himself saying the words out loud.

Fenrir turned, pushed Heimdall against the wall, and pressed his forearm to Heimdall's throat. "What did you just say?" He had misheard Heimdall's words, thinking that he'd said, "We're all going to die."

"They're all going to die," Heimdall repeated, gasping for air. "They've put them—women, children, the old, anyone who can't fight —in the dining hall. The fire's going to take them. They're all going to die if we don't get them out."

Fenrir realized his mistake and lowered his arm. "Sorry about that. I'm used to Aesir trying to kill me." Heimdall rubbed his throat. "Lead us up to the vantage point." Fenrir looked up and grabbed the closest soldier to him. "After that, take him and get them out through the tunnels."

Heimdall nodded. "Thank you."

"Don't thank me yet." He pulled Heimdall to his feet and gave him a small push forward. "Come on, lead the way."

CHAPTER FORTY-SIX

"Like cattle?" Modi gasped in disbelief.

"They outnumber us five to one," Magni chimed in, further emphasizing the ludicrousness of what he was hearing.

"Got any better ideas?" Lyfinder said. "Unless you can think of another way to evacuate twenty thousand people, all of whom think we're trying to kill them, I'm all ears." He scratched his wispy white beard. "I'm willing to bet it's complete bedlam there. I think it's meant to be late day now, but the sky's pitch black and the earth is shaking. What are we going to do? Walk in and say, 'Hello there, lovely to meet you, your realm's about to be covered in fire, won't you please follow us to safety, calmly and in an orderly manner'?"

The Jotunn army had reached the narrow pass, a thin strip of grassland that lay between Tilgrad and Pildur. They would soon split up, three thousand men to go with Magni and Lyfinder to Pildur (which had a population of twelve thousand) and the remaining two thousand five hundred to go with Modi to Tilgrad (which had a population of approximately eight thousand).

Just as with Jotunheim, and indeed all of Yggdra's inhabited realms, the towns had elders whom the townspeople would listen to. Loki's plan had been for Magni and Modi to talk with these elders directly, explain who they were. As the heirs to Asgard's throne, the elders would then be obliged to order the town's inhabitants to follow their command. "I've dealt with them many times in my youth," Loki told them. "They're reasonable men. If you explain the matter to them, they'll understand."

While he had no doubt that the elders would indeed turn out to be reasonable men, Lyfinder did not believe that, given the circumstances, the general populace would be in any condition to listen to them. He kept his opinion to himself, not wanting to question his newly found king's orders, but as they approached the two towns, he could not help but make his opinion known.

Rather than approach the town elders, Lyfinder argued, it would be better if the Jotunn army feigned an attack, pretending to pillage through the towns while in actuality guiding the residents like sheep toward the Iving.

Magni and Modi, who only two months ago had barely been trusted with caring for the blacksmith's shop, were now in the precarious position of leading the most massive evacuation the realms had yet to see. They stared at each other. Since birth, they'd been inseparable and had grown to know what the other was thinking simply by looking at them. They nodded in unison. "We stick to the plan," Modi said.

"As you wish," replied Lyfinder. "But don't say I didn't tell you so."

Bragi had been the chief elder of Tilgrad for well over fifty years. During that time, he'd come to believe that the wellbeing of Tilgrad had little to do with Asgard's benevolent monarchs. But that was before. Now he was convinced that the town would've been precisely as it was had Odin and Borr never existed. Then again, he thought, had they not existed, perhaps he wouldn't be where he was. Bragi had been elected to be an elder at the young age of forty-three, younger than any before, partly because someone—he didn't know who—had spread a rumor that he was Odin's distant relative. It wasn't true, of course, but Bragi wasn't about to let a simple thing like the truth get in the way of the most significant opportunity life had handed to him.

Under his watch, Tilgrad had grown from a squalor-ridden fishing town to the most renowned trading and cultural hub in all of Asgard. It wasn't an easy task, but nor was it as difficult as he'd imagined. The fairy story that he'd been a distant cousin (or uncle, or nephew; those who spread the rumors didn't have truth and accuracy on their mind) of Odin's had made traders throughout Yggdra want to trade with him.

The day had begun like any other, but then the ground started to shake, and soon enough, the sky had turned dark. "Ragnarok," Bragi mumbled to himself, recalling the lad who had arrived with a message from Mimir years earlier. As he'd prepared them to do, they rung the bell. Its ringing drifted throughout the town, informing Tilgrad's inhabitants that the time had come. They came rushing to the old man's house, and among them was a surprise Bragi had not anticipated: a Jotunn messenger.

Bragi scratched his beard, listening intently to the messenger's words. "Hmm," he said after the messenger had told him everything he had to say. "Thor's sons. That would explain his five-year disappearance." He sighed and grabbed a handful of soil from the earth. He placed it to his lips and gave it a gentle kiss. "Asgard, I have loved you, and I have served you, and now, for the sake of your people, I must abandon you."

Modi waited on the outskirts, more than two thousand men at his back. Bragi emerged from beyond the wooden fence surrounding the town. "Shall I call you sire?" Bragi said, his voice deep and far stronger than his body.

"You can call me what you wish," Modi said. "Up until two months ago, I'd been a smithy's ward, nothing more. I haven't built up the taste for big words and big titles yet."

"Jotunheim comes to Asgard's rescue, I hear. Have I heard correctly?"

"Loki Laufeyson spoke highly of you. Said you were a man of

intellect and principle. That you would listen to reason and do what is best for your people," Modi replied.

"And what is best for my people?" Bragi barked back, testing the young man.

"Life," Modi said. "Asgard is doomed. You know it. You've known it for years. You owe it to your people to lead them to safety. We welcome you to our home, not as guests, but as equals, just as entitled to it as we are."

Bragi smiled. "Those are not your words," he said, his voice full of fondness. "Those are the words of a friend I have not seen in many decades. I do not know you, and I do not trust you, but I know Loki, and I trust him. You may think of him as your king, but to me, he is something far grander. A good man." He furrowed his brow. "Your man told me that Thor had two sons, but I only see one."

"My brother, Magni, he's off with the rest of the army to evacuate Pildur."

Bragi gulped. His eyes widened. "Well, that's going to be a challenge."

───────────

The town of Pildur had about as much in common with its neighbor, Tilgrad, as a fruit fly has with a warthog. While Tilgrad had transformed from rags to riches, Pildur had gone from rags to even dirtier rags. This was in no small part due to its elders' philosophy. "Suffering breeds strength," they would say, and strangely, they were right. The vast majority of Asgard's military strength came from Pildur. Its men enlisted in droves, not because of their fierce loyalty to the crown, but because the town was such a stinking shit hole that the prospect of spending the rest of one's life training to die seemed like the more appealing option.

The elders of Pildur crowded around Magni and Lyfinder. Unlike Lyfinder had expected, the town hadn't been thrown into chaos. It wasn't that the tremors hadn't reached the town, or that the elders hadn't received Mimir's dire warning all those years ago, or that the raging fire spraying from the top of the mountain couldn't be seen. Rather, it was a longing toward an inevitable desolation, a craving for an end to the rigmarole, complete and utter boredom with life itself. Hydric, Pildur's chief elder, had once heard a man say, "I wouldn't mind if the world ended. It would be better than this place, anyway." The statement made him smile.

"What's wrong with them?" Modi whispered to Lyfinder. "Everything's going to hell, and they're acting like it's just another day."

Lyfinder scratched his beard and shook his head. "I'm trying to work that out myself." Had he known that all forms of joy and entertainment, such as playing games, listening to music, and storytelling, had all been long banned in the town; that there'd been a curfew, and every man, woman, and child was to be home before dark, he would've understood why the people of Pildur were reacting to the end of their world with all the energy of a sloth. It hadn't always been like this. During Borr's time, the town's elders had been under the king's control, and Borr prevented them from spreading their draconian doctrines. Odin, on the other hand, allowed them to do as they pleased, placing complete faith in their chief elder, Calsar. The king had no idea that Calsar, who was somewhat liberal in his leanings and beliefs, had died twenty-two years ago, allowing Hydric, the current chief elder, to do as he pleased, which meant employing strict and unpleasant measures.

"We come on behalf of Loki Laufeyson, the king of Jotunheim," Magni said. "Ragnarok is upon us. A fire that burns through this entire realm. We grant you and your people safe passage into Jotunheim. We welcome you to our home, not as guests, but as equals, just as entitled to it as we are."

"He's lying," squawked an old man with a squeaky voice. "It's a trap."

Hydric waved his hand at the man, quieting him. "I am an Aesir of Asgard. You are a Jotunn of Jotunheim. We are natural enemies. Had Odin's counsel been right and truthful, if indeed this Ragnarok is to plunge our realm in flame, surely Odin would have sent for us himself. Instead, we have you at our doorstep, sent to save us by the greatest trickster the nine realms have ever known."

"Should've gone with my plan," Lyfinder muttered under his breath.

Modi could not believe his eyes as the townsfolk marched out of their homes, an endless mass, moving like the tides of the sea. Jotunn and Aesir, side by side. Not silently—this was not a funeral march, after all—but conversing, turning the other into brother, two peoples morphing into one.

"They're just people," Bragi mused. "People with more in common than most would like to believe." Modi remained silent, awestruck by the sight of Aesir children climbing atop the shoulders of Jotunn soldiers. "We've been preparing for this for years, ever since we received Mimir Odin Counsel's letter. Madness and the inability to place people over self is a common thing in circles of power. However, I have personally met two men I can honestly say have not been struck by such an illness of the soul. Loki and Mimir, two shining lights in Odin's chasm of darkness. Although they might not be here, this is their work." He paused, knowing that as soon as he said what he was about to say, the calm of the moment would disappear. "We must go. The town of Pildur will not be as cooperative as ours. To its elders, suffering is a special form of joy. They do not understand reason or faith, only loyalty." He looked Modi in the eye. "I have a plan, but you're not going to like it."

"What is it?" Modi said.

The faint hint of a smile appeared on Bragi's lips.

"I'm beginning to think that you were right," Magni said to Lyfinder under his breath.

"Right now, speak," one of the elders said in a shrill voice. "Tell us why the bloody blazes we should follow you."

"Are you aware whom you are speaking to?" Lyfinder asked in a booming voice.

"Dirty Jotunn scum," said the elder with the high-pitched voice.

"This is Modi, son of Thor," Lyfinder said.

"Magni," Magni corrected him.

"This is Magni, son of Thor, rightful heir to the throne of Asgard."

"That's Modi," Magni said. "Modi's the heir."

"Apologies, sire," Lyfinder said quietly, but loud enough for the elders to barely hear what he was saying. "You both look so much alike. It's hard to tell you apart."

Hydric stepped forward. "And what, may I ask, is Thor's child doing leading a Jotunn army?" His eyes darted open. "Ah, now I understand. Thor must have had the urge when he was in Jotunheim. He was there for a long time, five years, I think—hot-blooded man, full of vinegar. You look like him, I'll give you that. But the bastard son of a Jotunn whore is not a legitimate heir."

"He's not a bastard," Lyfinder said matter-of-factly. He then quieted his voice. "You're not a bastard, are you?"

"Of course I'm not a bastard," Magni yelped. "Least I don't think so." He sighed. "Look," he said to the elders, pointing toward the faraway yellow glow, "that's a bloody mountain that blew its top off and it's spitting fire and farting so hard the earth's shaking. You got two options: stay here and die, or come with us and live with us as equals. Time's running out, so you better make your mind up fast."

Hydric snorted and spat on the ground. "I'm not convinced. Can't even prove that you're not a bastard. Besides, Odin's still alive, and he hasn't told us to go and follow some Jotunn army we've never seen before. So even if you are who you say you are, as far as I'm concerned, you ain't got no business telling me nothing."

Lyfinder rolled his eyes. "Can we finally go with my plan?" he said to Magni.

"What plan?" asked the elder with the high-pitched voice, his tone a cross between a bird chirping and a dog barking. "They got something up their sleeves. I don't like it," he said to the others.

"Not yet," Magni said, grinding his teeth. "But I am considering it."

A horn sounded in the distance. Magni recognized it. After all, it was his horn. The screeching pitch gave that away. He let out a small chuckle, remembering how he would often place it close to Modi's ears as he was asleep and blow as hard as he could. He'd managed to salvage the horn from the charred remains of the smithy's shop before they'd left Hurrugane, and gifted it to his brother. Although he couldn't understand what Modi might be up to, he understood why the horn had been sounded. It was a message, a message that only Magni would understand. *Buy time.*

The elder with the high-pitched voice began to pace. "I don't like it —not one bit. I don't like it. I don't trust 'em."

"What proof would you like?" Magni said. "I'm here to help you. Whatever you want me to do to prove to you that I'm truthful, tell me, and I'll do it."

"He hasn't attacked us," Hydric said, scratching his head. "He's got a lot of men."

"A lot," chimed in the elder with the high-pitched voice, still pacing.

"Yet he hasn't attacked." Hydric outstretched his arm, blocking the other elder's path. "Army that big, he could've wiped us out in an hour."

"You asking me to trust the bastard son of a Jotunn whore?"

"I'm not a bastard!" Magni growled.

"No, he's not!" called a deep, rumbling voice.

Modi emerged from the vast ocean of soldiers, sweat dripping from his brow, his horse gasping for air and an old man gripping his waist, holding on for dear life, hoping not to be blown away with the wind. They unmounted the steed. Had Modi not helped Bragi get down, the old man would've fallen flat on his face. At his age, riding no longer agreed with him. His face was yellow. The elder gripped his stomach, holding down what was about to come up.

"Odin's dead," Bragi lied. "Peace, that was his last wish. To finish his father's work. After all, Borr had only fought to end the endless fighting." He coughed at the bitter taste in his mouth. "Odin has fallen; the fire has claimed him," he gasped, placing a hand on Modi's shoulder. "Thor too. These young men are what remains of Borr's line." He took a deep breath and steadied himself. "Hydric, how long have you known me?"

"Too long to count," Hydric replied.

"And have I ever lied to you?"

Hydric shook his head.

"I am here to tell you that the realm is doomed. Mimir was right. If we do not escape, our people, those whom we swore to defend, will die. Before us is an opportunity to unite two peoples. Modi is, by law, our king. Not only that, but he is also the king of Jotunheim." Lyfinder's jaw dropped. Modi winked at him, wordlessly letting him know that this was a performance, nothing more than a white lie. "Two realms united under one leader," Bragi continued. "Borr's vision brought true."

Hydric rubbed his chin, but before he could speak, the elder with the high-pitched voice let his opinion be known. "I don't believe it. Lies, lies, and more lies."

"Silence," Hydric hissed. "We are loyal to the throne of Asgard. And we have witnessed that this young man before us is our rightful king." He lowered his head. "I would bow, sire, but my knees do not allow it."

Lyfinder began to count out loud. "One, two, three, four, five, six, seven." He looked at Bragi, and although they'd never spoken to each other before, they could tell what the other was thinking.

The crowd stood transfixed as the Jotunn army circled them. They ran out of their houses, left their shops unmanned, young and old, brave and scared, the easily bored and the easily amused. There were some whispers, but most of them just stared blankly, not knowing if the appropriate action was to run, surrender, fight, or celebrate.

The army had cleaved itself into seven contingents, each headed (or so it appeared to the masses) by one of Pildur's elders. It surrounded the town's borders, leaving no room for escape.

"This is going to work," Lyfinder said. "Just stick to the plan."

Hydric stood in front of the Jotunn elder. He swallowed, acutely aware of how dry his mouth was. "My brothers and sisters, Ragnarok has come." He rubbed his arm. "This day will be remembered. What you see before is not your enemy. For forty years, there has been animosity between the Jotunns and the Aesir, but today, as our worst fears are realized, as the world shakes and as the fire comes from the sky, let it be known that it was Jotunheim that came to our aid."

Due to their sheer number, the vast majority of the townspeople couldn't hear a word of what Hydric was saying. All the same, they stood to attention, not a soul among them uttering a single word. Just as Hydric was speaking, so too were the other six elders, telling their people that their time in Asgard was over; that the time of the Aesir had, at long last, come; that the Jotunns had accepted them into their land, not as guests, but as their equals.

While a number of the town's populace had extreme objections to what they were hearing, they kept those objections to themselves. After all, they had just learned that Modi Thorson, their rightful king, had marshaled the Jotunn army into Asgard. And who were they to question the wisdom of a king?

They took with them only what they needed and began the long walk to their new home. The two parties united on the banks of the Iving. All of them, twenty thousand Aesir and five and a half thousand Jotunns, crossed the frozen lake together. The ice cracked as their footsteps bore down upon it. But as they reached the other side, they saw a sight none of them had expected to see: A lone woman standing on the bank, her arm wrapped around herself, her blonde and grey hair an unruly mess atop her head, and dark circles etched around her eyes, which were red and filled with tears.

She scanned their faces, looking for the only family she had left, but Loki was nowhere to be seen. "Where is he?" Sigyn asked, her voice trembling.

CHAPTER FORTY-SEVEN

LOKI PICKED himself up off the blood-soaked soil. Arrows and balls of flame covered the sky. All around him, men, Jotunn and Aesir, scrabbled around, screaming to the heavens for mercy. His troops had pushed their way toward the wall of the castle, but could not yet reach it. Loki's boot sunk into the mud as he paced forward. The shield grew heavy in his arm. All around him, the Aesir ran, calling for mercy, begging the hell striking from above to end.

The arrows came heavy and in waves. As opportunity presented itself, Loki lowered the shield and counted the time between the barrages. *One, two, three.* A handful of Jotunns marched behind him. *Four, five, six.* He aimed, the shield weighing down his shooting arm. The shot flew upwards over the wall, arched, and bounced off the thick steel of the archer's chest plate. *Seven, eight, nine.* Hundreds of Aesir sprinted away from the battle, toward the forest. *Ten, eleven, twelve.* Loki raised his arm and closed his eyes. Shards of wood sprayed as the projectiles broke through the shield. Like clockwork, his arm came down, reaching for the quiver.

Bodies, most of them Aesir, began to pile up several feet away from the wall. Odin crawled over them. "Stop," he shouted to the archers, but the roars of desperation masked his cry. He pushed forward, pulled himself out of his men's clutches. "Get off me!" The arrow flew past his ear. He dropped to the ground before the second shot came. Their eyes met. *Twelve.* Another wave came, giving Odin the precious seconds he needed to dive between the corpses. Loki spat and looked up, counting, scanning for his target.

"Nock," said the commanding archer on the wall. *One, two, three.* They acted in unison, a well-oiled machine fulfilling its only function. "Draw." *Four, Five, Six.* There was an audible *hiss* as their bowstrings tightened. *Seven, eight, nine.* The archers aimed, their target anything that moved. *Ten, eleven, twelve.* "Loo—" Fenrir's arrow landed before the commanding archer could finish the word. It struck him in the back of the head and protruded from underneath his chin.

High atop the castle, from the balcony, the missiles came. "Fire at will," Fenrir commanded. There was a large *thrunk* as the men to his left and right fired. The shots landed across the wall. Archers ran for cover, lifting their shields above themselves, leaping down toward the castle's garden. There, they found no reprieve. The arrows followed them wherever they went, wherever they hid.

Fenrir lowered his bow as his men continued to shoot. The field beyond the castle was awash with death and fire. He couldn't see them clearly; there was no way to discern which of the men on the field were Aesir and which were Jotunn. He'd always believed war to be something clear, two sides with a line drawn between them, but as he stood on the balcony, desperately trying to find his father, he finally realized that there was no line. From that high up, both king and peasant were equal.

Odin dug his fingers between the hewn husks of meat that had once been his men, crawling, his body as low as his back would permit. He heard a scream behind him. Gasping for air, he turned. His blood-soaked fingers gripped the sword's hilt loosely. He thrust it upwards just as the Jotunn was about to descend upon him. The sword cut through the Jotunn's chest. Shards of broken bone, the man's ribcage, pried the blade from Odin's hands as the man fell. There was no one around, no one that might recognize him or care enough to risk life and limb for a man that might've spat at their existence. He climbed the wall with his eyes, looking for the archers that were supposed to be manning it.

The wall's parapets, which only moments ago had been filled to the brim, lay empty. The archers rushed toward the castle's entrance. Fenrir's men attempted to pick them off as they scurried down the winding road of the garden. They zigzagged, hid behind statues of men history has long forgotten, dived into the shallow waters of the garden's artificial ponds. "Damn it, Heimdall, where are you?" Fenrir said under his breath, not knowing that Asgard's Watcher was having —to put it mildly—a slight bit of difficulty convincing those huddled in the castle's dining hall to follow him.

Heimdall flung the great hall's sizeable wooden door open. Those inside stared at him blankly. "Come on then; we need to leave," he said. They would've listened to him had he not been accompanied by a Jotunn soldier; as soon as he entered, the blank stares on the faces of those in the hall were replaced by horrified expressions and screams of terror. "Wait," Heimdall said, "it's not what it looks like." They didn't listen, instead choosing to dart across the hall in every direction imaginable. "I'm trying to help you!"

A group of small boys huddled around the largest chair in the room, one with a seat so big it would take three men to fill. Odin's chair. They whispered an ill-conceived yet well-meaning plan and sprinted toward the door, screaming their little lungs out. They'd hoped to rush the Jotunn, to bury him with their weight. What courage they held in their hearts vanished the moment the Jotunn kicked the first of the boys to attack so hard he flew several feet into the air.

The Jotunn looked at Heimdall and winked. He then walked up to the largest of the boys and picked him up by the scruff of his shirt. The boy screamed, wailed, and kicked, his feet hitting nothing but air. "If you don't come with us," the Jotunn bellowed, "I'm going to cut this little runt in two. And after that, I'm going to cut the lot of you."

The commotion ended, and calm returned once more. Heimdall clapped his hands. "Alright, I need you to follow me in an orderly fashion. We don't have much time." The crowd huddled around him, seeking answers. Heimdall brushed their questions away and began to march toward the kitchen. His eyes fell upon a bottle of wine, open and half-drunk, sitting by the vegetable storage area. He snatched it, planning to finish its contents at a more appropriate time. *One swig for courage*, he thought as he placed the bottle to his lips. *Alright, maybe one more*. A rough hand snatched the bottle from his grip. The Jotunn gave him a deathly glare. He then leaned in, asking Heimdall to describe the route he would have to take through the catacombs, to guide the Aesir to safety.

"Behind me, and single file," the Jotunn said as Heimdall pushed aside the small cupboard covering the entrance. The Jotunn led the way, his hand planted on the cold, damp tunnel wall. Behind him, the (former) inhabitants of the castle grabbed hold of the person walking in front of them and waddled through the dark, away from the fighting and toward an uncertain future.

Heimdall sprinted through the endless passageways. The large wooden door, twenty feet high and wide, that had acted as the castle's primary entrance shook as he passed it. *Crash!* The lock came loose, snapping off from its hinges, as the men who were meant to be manning the wall came flooding in. They took one look at Heimdall and started after him.

He sprinted up the winding spiral staircase. Their footsteps echoed from behind and from below, an endless stampede. He tried to yell as he reached the balcony, but his lungs burned far too much.

"Get down!" Fenrir roared, his fingers curled up in a fist beside his head. Heimdall dropped to the floor. The Aesir flooded the pathway. Fenrir unclenched his fist and threw his arm forward. Arrows flew above Heimdall's head, taking out a substantial fraction of the oncoming Aesir horde. "Swords," Fenrir said, unsheathing his weapon and charging ahead. Heimdall sprinted forward, past Fenrir, onto the balcony.

Had the passageways been wider, the Aesir might've been able to encircle Fenrir and his men. Luckily, the passageway was less than fifteen feet wide. At such close quarters, the Aesir's numbers provided only a minor advantage, quick to be undone by their wounds, exhaustion, and the ferocity of Fenrir's troops. The Jotunns hacked them down as they scurried forward. Limbs cluttered the walkway as crimson pooled on the cobblestone floor. They beat them back, down the winding staircase. Then, the blast came.

The shockwave came with such viciousness that it shattered every window in the castle. Glass sprayed every which way. The force knocked Fenrir off his feet. He stumbled down the steps. Had it not temporarily incapacitated the Aesir, they would've surely cut him down. He wiped the stream of blood running down his forehead then weaved to the side as an Aesir's war hammer came down. Pushing himself up, he dove forward, planting his sword in the man's chest. They fell together, the dead toppling with the living. Fenrir looked up, expecting to see his enemy, but instead finding Heimdall's arm reaching out for him. "We need to get to the gate."

Outside, fire, fueled by molten stone, enveloped the horizon. The flame came gushing down the valleys, traveling as fast as sound, leaving nothing but death behind. Loki stared at it, as did every soul outside. He then lowered his gaze and fixed it upon his target. Odin clawed at the castle wall, screaming at the top of his lungs for someone to pull him up, to tell him why the arrows had stopped.

Loki fired. The arrow bounced off the thick metal of Odin's armor. The Aesir king dropped to the ground, crawling on all fours, looking for a weapon among the pile of bodies. His fingers landed upon an old war hammer. Loki ran forward, firing aimlessly. Odin shielded himself beneath the carcass of one of his soldiers. He gripped the hammer's handle as tightly as he could. Just as Loki was about to bring his sword down, Odin pushed himself up. The hammer connected with Loki's chest, throwing him backward. Blood flowed from his mouth. He spat it out and stood up.

Odin's arm was shaking. "Look what you made me do." His voice was a trembling wreck, broken by the weight of his shattered oath. "Look what you made me do!" Loki swerved as Odin swung madly. He reached for the quiver. Only three arrows remained. He took one out and dove to the ground as Odin turned again. The arrow pierced Loki's shoulder as he fell on it. He screamed, then bit his tongue. He pulled out another and quickly fired it. Once again, it bounced off of Odin's breastplate. Before he could react, the Aesir king grabbed him by the shoulder and thrust him upon the large wooden door barring the entrance to the castle, the force snapping the quiver's leather strap.

On the other side of the door, Fenrir charged. The Aesir scurried away like deer being chased by a lion. The Jotunn troops rushed atop the wall. Heimdall ran up to the lever and pulled. The castle's entrance flung open just as Odin's hammer struck Loki across the face. His nose cracked in upon itself. His teeth shattered, forming little knives that cut into the sides of his cheeks. "Look what you made me do," Odin shrieked. The next blow came to the chest, cracking the chest plate. "Look what you made me do." Blood clouded Loki's vision. Had he been able to see, he would've noticed Fenrir running toward him with all of his speed.

The sword struck Odin on the back. Sparks flew, but the blade was unable to pierce the dense covering. Odin flung the hammer. It hit Fenrir square in the chest. He flew backward, his sword leaving his hand as he landed on the moist earth. He reached out to grab it, but Odin's foot stomped down on it. Fenrir rolled out the way as the hammer hit the ground. Odin reached for the sword. He raised it high above himself and brought it down. The blade took flesh with it as it carved through Fenrir's thigh. Before his enemy could react, Odin pulled the sword back up and drove it through Fenrir's chest.

Loki, finally gaining sight of his surroundings from the bloody mess that had once been his face, screamed and charged. He tackled Odin to the ground, forcing the sword from his hand. Odin's fist collided with the bottom of Loki's chin. Blood sprayed as he fell and dropped Thor's hammer. He braced himself, stood, ran, kicked Odin down, and picked up the sword, not noticing Odin's tight grip on his son's hammer. Just as Loki was about to deliver the killing blow, severing Odin's neck from his body, the Aesir king hoisted up the hammer, knocking Loki to the ground.

King Odin stood above Loki, the hammer in his hand. "You made me do this," he said with tears in his eyes. "I didn't want to break the oath. You made me." The hammer came down, cracking Loki's ribs beneath it. "Look what you made me do!" Fenrir, with what little life he had left, reached for the quiver that had fallen off his father's back. A single arrow, one shot, but one shot was all he needed. Odin raised the hammer. "Look what you made me do!" he screamed.

The arrow pierced his right eye. Odin fell to his knees. He scanned the vista with his left eye, taking in the men running for their lives, bodies piled one on top of the other, the fire rushing toward them. "What have I done?" he said quietly. And those were the last words Odin, son of Borr, ever spoke.

Heimdall walked out from behind the castle wall, through the open wooden gate, and onto the field. All around him they ran, Jotunn and Aesir alike. "Abandon your posts," cried a distant voice. "The king is dead!" Not thirty feet from the entrance was Loki. Unrecognizable, his face a tattered rag of red, he was sitting cross-legged, rocking back and forth, his arms draped around the lifeless body of his son.

Loki rubbed Fenrir's hair. "I'm sorry," he said as he sobbed uncontrollably. "I'm so sorry." Heimdall approached him. He reached a distance where his voice might be heard but remained quiet. Loki looked up, and through the battered, mangled, fleshy mess, Heimdall could see the conviction in his eyes. He put a hand to the ground, grunting and grimacing as he pulled himself upright. "The stables," he said. "We have to get to the stables."

Heimdall lifted Loki's arm and placed it around his shoulder. Many of those running noticed them. The handful of Jotunn soldiers stationed at the wall abandoned their posts and made for their king. They marched alongside Heimdall, their hands to Loki's back. They made their way through the castle gate, past the water garden, and to the small horse stable that lay at the bottom of the castle.

The roaring fire from the mountain hurtled toward the castle, claiming the towns of Hurtil and Dilfir along its trajectory. Though Loki could not hear them, the men, women, and children of Hurtil and Dilfir screamed in agony as the flames licked flesh from bone.

Loki gripped the reins of the horse closest to him, pushing it into

Heimdall's hands. "Ride," he said, his voice sharp and clear despite his injuries. "Ride and never turn back."

Heimdall mounted the steed and outstretched his arm toward Loki. "Come on. We need to get you back home."

"But I am home," Loki said, smiling.

As Heimdall noticed the blood flowing freely from the cracks in Loki's breastplate, he understood.

"It's over," Loki said, not to Heimdall, but to himself.

Heimdall welled up. "It's been an honor."

"Oh Watcher of Asgard, watch over them. Thor's sons are your kings now. Their road will be long, and it will be hard. But you'll watch over them. Two peoples, forged into one. Watch over them."

Heimdall nodded, failing to hold back the tears flowing down his cheeks. "I will. I promise."

The horses galloped out into the black forest, their king behind them and destiny to their front. The weight hit Heimdall as he rode. The responsibility, the charge he'd been handed . . . the very thing he'd always sought.

Loki meandered through the winding halls of the castle, taking them in one last time. Memories came gushing forth, some painful, but many pleasant and wholesome. They bore down upon him, and after he'd had too much, Loki walked back out into the garden and onto the field.

He could hear it. The roaring drum of the coming fire. It did not scare him. He was ready. Loki looked up. His eyes saw past the mounds of flayed bodies to those waiting for him. The mother who died holding him in her arms. The father he'd never known. The teacher who loved him as a son. The brother he'd never had. The sons that fell in his arms. The wife that stood by him until her end. And as the fire enveloped him, a single thought permeated his mind.

"It was good."

EPILOGUE

Myths are peculiar things. It is often the case that the events that inspired them bear little to no relation to the stories shared by untold generations. But to look for factual accuracy in myth is to miss the point entirely. Stories that carry over through generations do so because they have something to say. While some venture off into the mythical world of the meta, asking us to question our existence, or the meaning of life, or some other such question that no one has an answer to, many tell us something about the simpler, but no less important, things in life: family, friends, good and evil, wrong and right and the grey that dances in between them.

So then, you might ask, what did this story have to say? That is a question you must answer yourself, for a story whose message is overt and written in bold font is no longer a story but a decorated sermon. Not that there is anything wrong with sermons, but personally, I am not a fan. Stories, in my humble opinion, are far more illuminating, that is all. They can be crude and dirty and unwieldly, but then again, isn't life?

The world's oldest living organism is a seemingly unremarkable bristlecone pine in California's White Mountains. It's just over five thousand years old. Our oldest stories are far older than that. Unfortunately, little evidence of them remains as they were, more often than not, passed down orally. Those stories echoed the tales of civilizations long forgotten.

Many have stated that Mesopotamia, which dates back more than ten thousand years, is the oldest civilization in human history. This is only a half-truth. It is the earliest *recorded* civilization in human history. It is not controversial to state that humans evolved from our archaic ancestors sometime around 315,000 years ago. However, it is controversial to say that humans did not spend the better part of three hundred millennia living like animals.

A great many civilizations were born and died during that sprawling span of time. It is just unfortunate that virtually nothing they built remains with us. Yggdra was one such civilization. As the majority of our species lived in caves and hunted for their next meal, Yggdra stood as a lone beacon of prosperity, privilege, and advancement in an uncivilized world. Thousands of years before the Mesopotamians developed what we call today cuneiform script, the nine realms of Yggdra filled entire libraries with books. Long before the Romans built their pipes out of toxic lead, the Vanir and Aesir had deemed the material hazardous and to be avoided.

No one knows how Yggdra fell. Whether it was a rapid decline, back into the barbarous ways of the hunter-gatherer, or whether it collapsed slowly, withering away. Some had theorized that Ragnarok had scarred their psyche to such an extent that every mountain became a Surt, ready to unleash its rage upon the world. In truth, it doesn't matter. What does matter is that it was there, shining its light alone in a sea of darkness. But now, only its stories remain. What will you do with them?

Your friend,
Hvedrungr

THE JOURNEY CONTINUES. . . .

Writing is a journey, and one of the most rewarding parts of that journey is building a relationship with my readers. I occasionally send out newsletters with details on new releases, special offers, and other bits of news relating to my writing.

By signing up to the mailing list, this is what you'll get:

1. You'll be the first to know about my upcoming books.
2. You'll get a free copy of the first two chapters of any of my future books.
3. You might be eligible to join my launch team (which means free books!).

Receive all of this and more by signing up at:
http:/mgfarija.com/

ENJOYED THIS BOOK? YOU CAN MAKE A BIG DIFFERENCE.

Reviews are the most powerful tools in my arsenal when it comes to getting attention for my books. As much as I'd like to, I don't have the financial muscle of a New York publisher. I can't take out full-page ads in the newspaper or put posters in the subway.

(Not yet, anyway.)

But I do have something much more powerful and effective than that, and it's something those publishers would kill to get their hands on.

A committed and loyal readership.

If you've enjoyed this book, I would be very grateful if you could spend just five minutes leaving a review (it can be as short as you like) on the book's Amazon page.

Thank you very much.

ABOUT THE AUTHOR

For as long as M.G. Farija can remember, he has been deeply passionate about stories, and that avid interest has stayed with him into adulthood. His debut novel, *Loki*, is a fantastical and emotive story. In it he pays homage to Norse mythology by writing it from the perspective of its most misunderstood character.

Printed in Great Britain
by Amazon